Make You Miss Me

L.A. SHAW

Copyright © 2022 by L.A. Shaw

All rights reserved. No part of this book may be reproduced, distributed, or transmitted in any form or by any means, without prior written permission from the publisher or author. Except for the use of brief quotations in a book review or as otherwise permitted by the U.S. Copyright Law.

This is a work of fiction. Names, characters, businesses, places, brands, media, events and incidents are either the products of the author's imagination or are used fictitiously. Any resemblance to actual persons, living or deceased, or events is purely coincidence.

Make You Miss Me

Editor: Brandi at www.mynotesinthemargins.com

Cover Design: L.A. Shaw - Canva

Formatting: L.A. Shaw - Vellum

Photo: Canva

✸ Created with Vellum

To all the dreams we never thought were possible...

Chapter One

Ashley

Nori Beach, North Carolina, is the calm to my normal New York City storm. Sitting on the breathtaking beach has me grateful for the time I get to spend here.

Luckily for me, every summer, when Lottie, the absolute best friend a girl could ask for, comes to visit her god-awful grandmother, I get to come spend a few weeks with her in this awesome tiny beach town.

My childhood bestie is beautiful and fun but sometimes she doesn't always know how to show it, which is what she has me for… her number one fan.

This past Tuesday, we met a few hot guys while on the boardwalk. They were talking non-stop about this badass Halloween-themed summer party coming up. That piqued my interest, and when they said it wasn't until this weekend, I knew that would give me enough time to design, shop and piece together two sexy as sin playboy bunny outfits.

My love for fashion design began the summer my nana taught me to thread a needle and work her sewing machine, and it hasn't wavered since. There is something about seeing my ideas and designs in real life that brings me such an accomplished feeling. And let's be real, are you really living if you don't dress up like you're part of the "I love Hugh Hefner gang" at least once in your life?

Convincing Lottie to wear it was another story. Her curves in this outfit... I mean damn, if I wasn't strictly dickly, I'd totally do her.

She looks fucking hot! And once she saw how snatched her body looked in the outfit, her face lit up. You can see it in her eyes, the confidence she possesses in this costume with her banging body and gorgeous face. Lottie embodies her nickname to its fullest. Tig Ol' Bitties, aka Tig, because her titties are always on full display, even when she tries to hide them.

I'm feeling like a little vixen myself, with my freshly dyed blonde hair. It's quite the drastic change from my natural brunette, but I love the way it makes my blue eyes pop.

Currently, my long hair is curled in loose beach waves, falling down my back. I didn't go too heavy on my eye makeup because we wore fake lashes in true Playboy Bunny fashion. I threw on some lip stain and bronzer to complete my look. Thanks to my Italian heritage, I have gotten a nice tan quickly this week.

I would consider myself a confident chick, but as most of us ladies do, I have my days where my insecurities take up way too much space in my head... but not tonight. Tonight, we look hot as fuck, and I'm ready to flaunt it. Especially after the pre-game shots we just took.

We walk into the massive house party like we own the place. If there is one thing my father taught me I agree with, it's a strong poker face and a shit ton of confidence can get you a long way.

Who cares if we don't know anyone here?

Grabbing a beer, we head to the dance floor. So many eyes are on us, but I can't stop staring at the intense green pair watching me from the corner. There is such familiarity in those hypnotizing eyes. The Joker makeup he's wearing hides his face, and I can't tell the color of his hair underneath the green spray, but he looks hot as hell staring at me from the other side of the room.

Before I even saw his eyes, I could feel him. It was as if his mind conspired with my own and forced me to look his way.

I turn my attention back to my girl right as she drops it low and seductively drags her ass back up my front. Within a few minutes, a group of guys surround us. None of which grabs my attention.

Not giving them the time of day, I continue to dance with Lottie until I hear a husky voice. "I had to move quickly with all the other hungry eyes in the room on you. I'd hate to break someone's hand for touching you first." Leaning into him as his hand travels from my elbow to my hips.

His husky, possessive words turn me on more than I have been in months.

Not wanting to break girl code, I eye Lottie to see if she minds if I dance with him for a bit. She gives me a knowing smile and steps outside to get some air.

My body molds to his as we grind on the dance floor. This guy knows how to move.

Dragging Lottie to this party was supposed to be about getting her out of her shell in this amazing beach town. I didn't think it would be about me and this electrifying feeling the Joker is giving me as I rub my bunny tail all over his hard body on the dance floor.

This reaction my body is having to him… I've only had one other time and if it wasn't so far-fetched, I would wonder if it could be *him*. But I quickly shake off that feeling. *Forget about it, Ash.*

My lust for him is consuming me and I honestly don't give a fuck who is watching as we dry hump each other to the beat of each song.

Dipping his head down to my neck, he licks his way from my collarbone to my ear. My throat releases a deep moan.

After several songs and some heavy petting, he groans, spins me around, grabs my ass, and pulls my front into his hard bulge. "I have to have you, Doll. Please tell me I can taste this sweet pussy of yours."

I don't answer with words. I look into his green eyes, now dark as the sea at night, and he smirks at me. Probably seeing the answer in my lust-filled stare.

I go up on my tiptoes and lick his bottom lip. He moans, then takes control and devours my mouth.

Fuuuck, not only does this turn me on, but it also has sparks firing all over my body.

Before I can think more about that, I grab his hand to pull him outside.

"Hey, where we goin'… This is my house. I gave the guesthouse to my cousin for the night, but we can go upstairs to my old room for some privacy if you want… Shit, I hope you want that."

I let go of his hand and grab his pants by the waistband, skimming my fingers along the top of his boxers. "Oh, you're getting it… but first, I have to tell my hot date where I'm heading off to."

He shakes his head, chuckling, obviously knowing I mean the sexy bitch I came through the door with tonight.

Once outside, we make our way across the large patio. There are groups of people everywhere, all laughing, drinking, and smoking. At the far end, we spot my little bunny friend huddled up, talking with a jacked batman, and make our way in that direction.

The Joker, ironically enough, startles Batman, who appears to be entranced by every word my girl is saying to him.

What are they feeding these boys around here? Must be something in the water at Nori Beach because seeing them stand beside each other… damn those are two fine specimens.

I love seeing how Batman is eating out of Lottie's palm and seems to only have eyes for her. I think we may have interrupted something between them, which excites me even more. That is so unlike Lottie, but she needs to take more chances and let her freak flag fly.

We tell them we're going to dip out to go chill for a bit, keeping the convo short since Lottie, to my surprise, seems eager to hang with her newfound friend, which earns her a whisper from me.

"Forget about that douche, Jonathan, for the night. Honestly, Tig, you don't owe him anything."

I kiss her on her flushed cheek and then I'm being pulled away by the hot, mysterious Joker.

Minutes later, we bust through what I assume is his bedroom door. I've had little time to scope out the house because I've been too focused on much better things.

I'm in his arms, koala style, with my legs wrapped around him and my pussy rubbing on the very hard, very thick bulge in his jeans stretching up to his stomach.

Not sure if it's the shots I downed while getting ready earlier or if it's just him making me extra brazen tonight. Either way, I know I am of sound mind and want him so badly I can taste it.

Please get that thing inside of me.

He growls and I realize I must have said that out loud when he puts me down to rip my bunny tail bottoms down and says, "You don't have to tell me twice, Doll."

There's that familiar feeling again... But before I can think more about this nagging feeling, I'm being pushed up against the wall.

"Put your legs over my shoulders... I'm going to fuck you, but first I'm getting a taste."

Holy shit... yes please!

Like the good girl I am, I do as I'm told.

The way he admires my pussy has me feeling every bit the sexy vixen I want to be tonight.

"Damn, I can just look at this pretty pink cunt dripping for me and know you're going to be my new favorite meal."

As if I wasn't already about to die from his words alone, he tilts and slowly spits on my sex, which has got to be the hottest thing I've ever witnessed in my life.

I let out a guttural moan when he fucks me with his mouth. Licking me from bottom to top. If his dirty talking didn't tell me he knows what he's doing, he proves it by playing with my clit and showing it the attention it deserves. His devotion to my pussy has my body already tightening up with impending release. "Oh fuck, I'm about to come!"

He must be trying to make jokes because he stops with one last lick up the center of my slit. Before I can kill him for denying me, he says, "I want you to come on my cock. I want to feel this sweet pussy of yours clench around me."

At that, he rips his pants and boxers down and I finally get to see the complete package, and let me just say, it does not disappoint.

I gawk at him because, duh, what else can a girl do?

His face turns into a deviant smirk as he walks over to his bedside table with his dick practically saluting me. I must look crazed because he chuckles, "Why so serious?"

I almost miss the reference, too busy salivating over the sight of him rolling the condom on. I come to my wits and smirk back at him. "Give me all you've got, Mr. J."

He accepts the challenge and picks me back up, slamming me against the wall. I love that we're so into one another that we can't even make it past this part of his bedroom.

Within seconds, he has my body and mind filled with him.

"Fuuuck baby, you feel so good," he moans into my mouth before he kisses me, intertwining his tongue with mine, reminding me exactly what his licks are capable of and why I'm already so close to coming.

"Yesss right there, don't stop... ohhh shit, yess!"

He's right on my g-spot when he stops kissing me and starts to rub my clit. My body is like a live wire.

"Good girl… that's right, give it to me."

Those words put me over the edge he's had me hanging on since the dance floor, and I've never felt so unbelievably euphoric in my life.

I don't even know what I'm saying or moaning because I can't control the power this orgasm has over me.

Hearing his moans and seeing his green eyes turn almost black as he chases his own release has my pussy clenching around him again. Even with his slightly smeared face paint on and green hair, he is so fucking hot he makes my heart stop.

Holy fuck, did that really just happen?

"Oh, fuck babe, what did you just do to me?" he says as he leans down into my neck.

He's holding up all my weight and I can't even answer him, but I'm wondering the same exact thing. I guess he understands my sated silence because he says, "I have no fucking clue what that was, but I do know I'm not done with you yet."

Then he stands back up to his full height of at least six-four and holds me close as he carries me over to his bed and tosses me down.

I let out a squeal, and he leans down to give me a quick kiss on the mouth before stepping away to throw the condom out in the bathroom.

Lying here in my spot of orgasmic bliss, I notice little things around his room. I see a framed jersey with what I assume is his last name — "Manning"—and the number 59 across the back. *Of course, he plays ball.*

There are two academic awards on a shelf that grab my attention. Dude looks like that and he's smart… damn, what a catch. Too bad I—*stop Ashley, let yourself have tonight!*

Leaning up to see the awards, I'm hoping they have his name on them because I just had the best sex of the century and don't even know his name.

Of course, they don't, only the award's title and the academic year, just my luck.

Coming out of the bathroom with a washcloth in his hand, he gently cleans up the mess he's made between my thighs. He winks at me and walks back into the ensuite, but leaves the door open. I watch as he wipes some of his own smeared makeup while looking in the mirror.

"Damn, I forgot I had this mess on my face. Good thing it's the good shit." He smirks at me through the reflection.

Walking back over to his nightstand, he proceeds to grab a golden strip of condoms and throws them onto the bed, letting me know exactly what his intentions are.

Rolling his body on top of mine, he growls into my neck, "Fuck, you feel like mine." He kisses and nips at the sensitive skin along my neck and throat. Marking me as his... at least for the night, and I'm loving every second of his attention.

Kissing his way to my tits that are spilling out of the top of my corset, he licks the exposed mounds, pulling down the top of my costume and freeing my nipples.

"Fucking perfect." He groans into my chest while I writhe beneath him, unable to control my want for him.

He takes one of my nipples into his mouth and teases the hardened bud with a flick of his tongue. I moan at the contact.

"Mmm," I continue to moan as he gives both the girls special attention.

Grabbing the back of his head, I pull him up to my face. Our lips collide in a frenzy of passion. Fuck me, this guy is going to be the death of me.

"I want you on all fours, baby."

Flipping me like I weigh nothing, he positions me on my hands and knees. I let out a gasp at the sudden movement but quickly bounce back with a shake of my ass in his direction, letting him know I'm ready for whatever he's got for me.

He whispers, "Fresh little minx." This time, I grind my ass back into his hard dick.

And as if he can't wait another second, he starts untying the back of my corset. I love that I'm driving this sexy-as-fuck guy so wild with lust.

"Aren't you the perfect little present I get to unwrap? I can't wait to see these beautiful tits of yours bounce as I ride you hard… Can you handle that, my little bunny?" He gives my wiggling ass a quick slap.

"Oh God, yes!" I moan, unable to form any other words because my anticipation for round two has all the blood rushing to my core and none to my head.

Still pulling at my corset laces, he leans down to my ear and whispers, "No, not God, but close… it's Trent, and that's what I want to hear you scream when I make you come from now on, Doll."

My heart drops to my stomach.

Wait, what…

Every tingle, every spark…

Everything makes sense now.

Trent

Fuck man, I'm ready to take this girl again. Her heavy breathing and the way she's rubbing her thighs together as I untie her corset proves she is just as ready as I am.

There's something so familiar about her, like I've had my hands on her before. Maybe the tequila from earlier is hitting a little harder than I thought.

I don't know if it's the feeling of familiarity or what, but damn, she already has me addicted after one quick fuck against the wall.

We've been so caught up in each other we haven't even exchanged names, but for round two I plan to take my time, and I want to hear my name when she's moaning in pleasure.

I lean down, untying the last of her corset allowing it to fall to the bed, and whisper, "No, not God, but close… it's Trent, and that's what I want to hear you scream when I make you come from now on, Doll."

I feel her body, which was just putty under my touch, tense up. *What the hell?*

Trying to bring her back to me, I gather her long hair from her back and wrap it around my fist. In doing so, I reveal a gorgeous tattoo running down her spine.

I run my fingertips along the words and trace the design at the top. *No, it couldn't be.*

"Maggie?" I question.

That's when everything seems to hit her, and she scurries away from me.

"Whoa, what's wrong, babe? I can't believe it's you!" I smile widely at her. *What are the chances?*

Taking a step back, I admire her bare form. "Wow… I haven't stopped imagining what you would look like stripped down for me. Now, seeing you standing here without that sexy mask and outfit, the reality is far better than I envisioned. You're fucking stunning."

Except this blonde Maggie does not look happy to see me, even though I've been dreaming about this day for months. That's when it hits me. She tensed up when I told her my name.

"I… I'm… I'm sorry I have to go. Fuck, I'm so sorry Trent," she says, while trying to gather her clothes.

"What's wrong? Why are you running?" I reach out for her, but I can tell my comforting words won't change what's happening. It's like an ice-cold bucket of water has been dumped on me. What the hell is going on?

She has tears in her eyes as she attempts to re-lace her corset, her trembling fingers missing the loopholes.

Seeing how upset she is, I don't want to cause her any more distress, so I hand her a t-shirt that will be long enough to cover her ass.

She grabs it and slides it over her gorgeous body. "Thank you, Trent." She hurries towards the door. "I'm so fucking sorry." These are the last words she says as she walks out the door, closing it gently behind her.

What the fuck just happened? Feeling like déjà vu all over again, but this time it was even worse because she chose to leave me.

Chapter Two

Trent

5 MONTHS EARLIER

Walking into Masqued, the excitement along with the lust in the room is palpable.

This club is sick. The main area is set in the center of the place with views from the upper two floors. Iron and glass railings leave an open view for members to see the shows below from all areas of the building. The tall walls are covered with deep red curtains that match the intricate iron and wood furnishings that take up most of the open main floor.

Sexy-ass chicks walk around serving the patrons drinks, socializing, and dancing. Everyone here is disguised in a mask which only adds to the overall sex appeal of this place.

At first, I tried turning down my older brother's offer to spend my birthday weekend with him in New York City. I didn't want to leave my boys and my hookups behind because what else would make an eighteenth birthday special? Sorry, but let's be honest, I am a teenage Bo—nope, a teenage man now and of course, our birthdays must consist of the Fantastic Four.

Bros, Booze, Blunts, and Booty.

But Trevor promised me a wild night at an unforgettable club with way more ass than I could handle.

So of course, I said, "Count my ass in."

We walk up to the end of the long bar where my brother is welcomed with a wide, flirtatious smile from the bartender. She greets him like an old friend. "What's up handsome… You want your usual?"

My brother nods and says, "Thanks, Cass."

Cass looks at me, then her eyes drop to my wrist and the wristband that tells the world I'm not twenty-one yet.

Trevor speaks up when the bartender remains silent. "Cass, this is my younger brother, Trent. We're celebrating his eighteenth birthday, hence the wristband."

I put on my best smile, hoping like hell she'll ignore the band and serve me a beer.

"Oh no, I don't think so… That southern boy charm won't work on me." She smiles back, giving my brother a wink as she does.

This club is so upscale there's a yearly membership fee, which allows members to bring guests. If the guests are underage, they must wear a discreet black band. Everyone, including the employees, has on masks which gives this place even more of a forbidden feel.

I didn't understand why Trevor handed me a mask before we got here, but now it all makes sense.

Masqued may be full of people half-dressed and ready to fuck, but you can tell they run a tight ship that requires their clients to have deep pockets. The fact my brother can afford a membership here and the penthouse he has in Manhattan solidifies the fact that he's doing more than working for a private practice.

I've always looked up to my brother. I wanted to be a doctor just like him and our father, but I see myself more in the hospital setting, directly at the bedside, helping people. I'd be kidding myself if I didn't admit to the appeal of his lifestyle.

My parents thought it was strange when he left the hospital one year into his career after his residency, claiming to work for a private practice, but after seeing how he lives this weekend, something doesn't quite add up. I ain't saying shit, though. It doesn't directly affect me, and he's a grown-ass man. I'm just curious.

I turn back to the bar and catch Cass smirking at me as she pours the blue label Johnny Walker into the glass. "Well, there is plenty of fun to be had here with or without alcohol. Happy birthday, little brother!"

Trying hard not to stare at her tits, I thank her and turn to look around the room while Trevor continues making small talk with her.

No one is on the large center stage just yet. Trevor told me the main event starts in about thirty minutes.

Several lap dances are going on around the room. Some of the Masqued girls are at the tables hanging with the other parties, mostly made up of men, but there are plenty of women members here too.

Members are hanging out on the upper floors as well, sipping cocktails while overlooking the booths and bustling main floor below them.

I'm particularly interested in what's going on down the hall that runs behind the main stage. I've noticed multiple guests disappear that way, especially the couples.

The need to know what's back there has me wanting to leave my brother behind.

I'm snapped out of my thoughts by a sexy voice. "Hey Cass, you got table fifteen's drinks ready?"

I don't even hear Cass respond because I look over and see the most beautiful set of blue eyes looking back at me. She's wearing a lacelike black mask that's decorated with hanging jewels. The way it contrasts with her cerulean gaze makes her eyes so hypnotizing.

She looks younger than Cass, maybe even around my age, but it's hard to tell because I can't see her full face. Fuck me... I can see her nipples through her thin lace top. Damn that outfit. It's like lingerie but a dress, all black and fucking perfect on her.

She is breathtaking... Literally. I feel like I can't breathe. *Get your shit together, pussy.*

The brunette beauty holds my stare until Cass places the drinks on her tray and says, "Here ya go, Mags!"

Mags, as Cass calls her, walks away, and I have to make myself stay rooted to the bar so I don't chase after her. I have never felt whatever that was when our eyes locked before in my life.

"For fuck's sake!" I huff out loud, now noticing even more of her body as she walks away.

She has on these cheeky shorts you can see through the sheerness of her dress, showcasing her juicy ass. The top of the dress is backless, with no bra in sight, just like I expected. Down the spine of her back is a tattoo I can't make out right now, but it's some type of lettering and sexy as fuck.

She sways her hips as she walks away, and my eyes follow every step she takes in her fuck me heels.

My dick was already stirring in my pants at the first sight of her, but right now, as she turns around and looks back at me one more time, I have officially gone into gotta-have-her mode.

I turn to my brother with a huge smirk on my face, "I know exactly what you can get me for my birthday."

He grins with a knowing smile. "I'll see what I can do. I've seen her around, but never seen her doing anything other than waitressing."

Surprisingly, I like that answer, even if it means I don't get what I want. From one look at her, I can't stand the thought of anyone else having her.

Cass speaks up and Trevor looks to her for an answer. "Yeah, Maggie doesn't typically do private sessions or stage work."

I speak directly to the bartender. "Will you please see what it will take to get her to have a one-on-one with me? She already rocked my world with one look. I can only imagine what being with her in private would be like." I see her eyeing me like the pathetic fool I'm acting like, but I can't help it. The need to have my hands on her is overwhelming. "I'm not opposed to begging."

My brother chuckles "Damn baby brother, did she put a spell on you in that thirty seconds y'all were eye fucking each other?"

"Honest to God, I think so."

Cass tells us to go relax for a bit and she'll see what she can find out.

My right leg won't stop bouncing with anticipation, waiting for Cass to come back. There are so many fine girls here and several have stopped by our table to chat with us.

I can't be the only eighteen-year-old dude who comes to a place like this and gets pussy struck by some chick within minutes of being here.

Finally, she comes back, but instead of addressing both of us, she sits on Trevor's lap and whispers in his ear. I'm wondering if there is more to these two because my brother hasn't had eyes for anyone else tonight either.

I am waiting with bated breath as they continue to whisper.

Hurry the fuck up.

Trevor nods his head, and a big grin spreads across his face.

She kisses him on the cheek, stands up, and says, "Okay little brother, come with me."

Hell fucking yeah, I practically have to stop myself from fist-pumping the air.

Patting Trevor on the shoulder as I pass him, I say, "Thanks. You're the best brother a guy could ask for."

"Just don't embarrass me and jizz in your pants after two minutes."

That makes me chuckle, but honestly, if there was ever a chick that could make that happen, this is the one.

I follow Cass down the hall that had me intrigued earlier and find it has a bunch of private rooms. Most of the doors are blacked out, so I assume several intimate dances are going on, but then we pass one with partially frosted glass that you can see inside. A tall dark-haired guy is getting head from a blonde... Well, damn, there's a bit more than private lap dances going on back here.

Cass speaks up. "Don't get any ideas. Those two are a couple. Couples can choose to use these rooms and do whatever they want in them, with or without an audience."

Well, that answers that.

Cass opens a door at the end of the hallway and tilts her head for me to follow. It's a small room with dark red velvet curtains lining the walls, just like the rest of this place. In the center of the room sits a large, tall, high-backed chair with a small round table next to it. The lighting is dim but not dark enough that you can't see what's going on.

"Make yourself comfortable." Cass gestures to the large chair.

"Thanks, Cass, I owe ya one. Well, maybe Trevor does." I wink at her and sit my ass down in the chair.

Fuck, this is crazy. I've never been this anxious about a chick before. There's just something about her, the way she looked at me. Shit, I'm already hard just thinking about it.

"Now listen up playboy, Maggie doesn't normally do this type of thing, so go easy on her. This shit is on her terms. If she wants to stop, you stop." I nod in anticipation.

"You do not touch unless you ask, and she gives you verbal consent... and absolutely no sex." My eyebrows furrow at that. I thought this place was a sex club. I open my mouth to ask, but she takes the words right out of my mouth.

"This is not a sex club, this is an exotic club. Plus, that shit is illegal in New York." She winks at me, smiling. "Enjoy yourself youngin'. She's a feisty one."

"Thanks, Cass... honestly."

She walks out mumbling something under her breath, but I can't make it out. I'm too distracted by the song that starts to play through the speakers. It's a slow, sensual beat.

The door opens and Maggie steps in. Biting her lip nervously. Shit, I hope she wants to be here as much as I want her to be. She makes eye contact with me and smirks. Thank fuck, I knew she felt it earlier, too.

I sit forward in my chair, waiting for her to get closer. *Come on, Doll, I'm not going to hurt you.* She approaches my chair with a sway to her hips and I'm about two seconds from throwing Cass' rules right out the window. This girl is sexy as fuck, and she knows damn well what she's doing to me.

Maggie steps between my spread legs and places her hands on my shoulders.

"Hey." She smiles down at me.

"Hey, beauty."

Just as the chorus drops in the song, she turns around and straddles my lap. Giving me the perfect view of her round ass. I go to grab a handful and clench my hands into fists. *Show some restraint.*

She grinds her ass along my dick, and I let out a groan. Fuck, she feels perfect. The way her hips move, I can't help but move along with her.

"That's it Doll, rub that sweet pussy of yours all over my lap." She shudders at my words.

Maggie repositions herself so she is now leaning her back against my chest. Dropping my head to the crook of her neck, I breathe in her intoxicating scent.

"Please tell me I can touch you, Maggie. I'm dying over here."

"God yes, I was wondering what the fuck you were waiting for, handsome!" She yelps as I grab hold of her hips and slow her rhythm.

The music changes to a slower song and my girl doesn't skip a beat. Her movements are more fluid and sensual the longer the song plays.

I slide my hands up her torso. "Is this okay?" I don't want this shit to end, so I want to make sure she is comfortable.

"Yes, please keep touching me. I need your hands on me."

I wrap my hands to the front of her body, lightly skimming the exposed skin in her dress. She moans as I continue exploring her perfect curves. My fingers graze across her hard nipples and she pushes her chest into my hands.

Shit. I can't believe I'm not allowed to fuck this chick. This is the biggest cock tease of all time. What I wouldn't give to be buried deep inside her right now.

I pinch her nipples gently as she grinds on me. Her breathing is heavy, and I think my girl is getting off on this. *And here I thought I would be the one to bust too soon.*

I move her long, brown hair off her shoulder and kiss her neck, testing the waters.

"You like that?"

"Fuck yesss," she moans out. God, if she keeps moaning like that, I will come. *Get your shit together.*

I lean back into the seat to get the full visual of this gorgeous chick on me. I move her hair again so I can make out what the tattoo says on her back. In a very delicate script down her spine are the words "Even in darkness there is light" with a moon design on top. Not really sure what it means to her, but it's pretty fucking sexy.

Goosebumps erupt over her skin as I trail my fingers along her spine.

"What's your name?" she questions with a heavy breath.

Needing to see this girl come undone before my eyes, I lift her dress slightly and help her flip around so she's facing me while she grinds against my dick.

"Aww, you want to get to know me better, Doll?" I say as I grab her hips and drag her over my throbbing cock, making her gasp when I hit my intended target. "It's Trent, so you can say it out loud when I make you come in a minute."

"Oh, fuck," she says, circling her hips on me.

"That's it… give it to me." I practically growl into her ear. I continue dragging her body over my lap, kissing and nipping at her neck. Her body quakes, and I know this girl is about to come undone for me.

"Oh, fuck… fuck Trentttt," she screams out as her body convulses on me.

"That's a good girl," I say as I continue to kiss along her shoulder. Her body flutters with aftershocks while I sit with the most smug-as-fuck look on my face. I did that to her. I made her come undone like this.

She grabs my face and kisses me. I wasn't expecting it, so it takes me a moment to realize what she's doing. But as soon as

I do, I grab the back of her head and deepen our connection.

Her tongue intertwines with mine in the most delicious way. There is no way this chick is real. I need more of this. Whatever this is, I need more.

There's a knock on the door and a gruff voice radiates through. "Times up Maggie."

What? Already? It feels like it's only been a few minutes, not a half-hour.

She pulls away from me and smiles, "Thanks for that…" She climbs off me and adjusts her dress. Fuck! This can't be over. I need more time.

"Wait… Give me your number, beauty. I need more time with you."

She lets out a laugh. "I'm sorry, only one private dance per night. It's a rule."

"That's not what I meant. I mean outside of here. Anywhere… fuck."

She turns to head towards the door.

"This was amazing… seriously, thank you," she says over her shoulder when her hand reaches for the doorknob.

And then she's gone.

Chapter Three

Ashley

Present

Standing beside the iron gates that lead to Trent's massive property, I stare mindlessly at my phone. Hoping like hell I didn't ruin anything for her. Lottie deserved this night, and I had to go and mess it up with my freak out.

I had no choice. When I heard 'Maggie' I froze, and my instinct was to run.

Come on, Tig, I gotta get out of here. My leg is twitching, and my skin is crawling to get away.

Thankfully, I'm hidden by the shadows of the large trees that line his property. Otherwise, I think people would look at me funny. Especially considering I'm standing here in Trent's oversized t-shirt and my hooker heels. His smell surrounds me, and I can't help but wrap my arms around myself, imagining it was him with me. How I wish that were true.

Fuck! Of course, it would be Trent and here, of all places. I knew I recognized those eyes and the way my body came alive under his touch. I stare up at the sky and laugh maniacally, "You sure do have some sense of humor."

I let out a deep sigh of relief when I hear footsteps approaching. "Bitty!" is all she gets out before wrapping her arms around me and bringing me in for a hug.

"I'm okay, babe," I whisper into her shoulder. "I just needed to get out."

"What did that fucker do? I'll knock him out," Lottie questions as she pushes back to evaluate my current state.

"I'll tell you, but can we get out of here first?" I don't even recognize the weak-sounding voice that leaves me.

"Okay, let's go. Should we stop and get some more beer? Are we going to need more alcohol for this?"

"No, I'll be fine. Maybe a joint?" I laugh as we lean against an enormous tree trunk.

I look over at my bestie and smile. Thank fuck for her. Honestly, she's the best. I know I'm in my own shit right now, but I can't forget to ask her about Batman and what transpired that *she's* now dressed in *his* t-shirt.

"Hey, do I need to call us an Uber?" I question as we stand together.

Moments pass in pure silence. I look at Lottie to make sure she heard me, but she's staring off into space.

"Helloo, earth to Lottie. Girl, are you dickmatized already?"

Snapping to, she laughs while shaking her head. "Oh shit, sorry. No, I called us one right after you texted. Should be here any minute." A huge smile spreads across her face as she adds, "You know what I might be."

The Uber pulls up shortly after, and the ride to her house is only 5 minutes. Lottie doesn't press me for answers since we're amongst unknown company. It's a given we'll wait to dish out all the deets when we're home. Both of us just enjoy the quiet ride in our own little worlds.

We make our way up her long driveway with our arms intertwined. Thank goodness Ethel isn't home to witness this debauchery. We look like complete trash staggering towards the house in our oversized men's t-shirts and high heels.

After smoking an expertly rolled joint, thanks to yours truly, we collapse on the oversized bed in Lottie's room. Making ourselves comfortable, we tear into our snacks.

"Mmm… I fucking love you." I moan as I take another handful of popcorn.

"I know!" She shoots me a wink and shakes a bunch of M&M's into her bowl. She then pours some of the popcorn into it as well. I am mortified as she proceeds to eat the combination in one go.

"That's weird." I scrunch my face as she continues to munch.

"I'm high as shit, and this is delicious." She laughs as she rolls onto her back.

"So how was he?" I question, looking at the smile on her face, knowing damn well it was Batman who put it there.

"You want me to go first?" She lifts her eyebrow, giving me her best 'I know what you're doing' smirk.

"Ugh, I'm not ready yet." I sigh in defeat as I drop onto my side to face her.

She looks at me intently. "Are you sure, babe? I don't want to go on about my night when I know how yours ended."

Again, this is why I fucking love this girl. "No, I promise I'm okay. It's not that it ended poorly… It's just a lot more complicated than I was expecting."

She sighs deeply and begins retelling the events of her time with Greyson. By the look on her face, I can tell it truly was something special. Good, I'm glad. This girl needs some positive attention. Fuck knows everyone else in her life besides me blows.

I gasp as she tells me his reaction to Jonathan's text. Hot damn! Next time I see Greyson, I'm going to give him a high five. The fact that her so-called 'boyfriend' bashed her for her costume makes my blood boil.

Jonathan's a prick. She deserves so much more. I'm thankful "G"—as Lottie is now calling him—was there to tell her the truth. She's absolutely stunning.

Unfortunately for her, the T-shirt was just a friendly gesture. Too bad, my girl could certainly use a release, even if she'll never admit to it.

I roll onto my back as she continues her story. I can't help my thoughts from wondering about Trent…

---

5 MONTHS AGO

Walking out of one of the rooms at Masqued, a room I swore I would never go in, with my head held high because dayum… That certainly was worth it.

The intrigue won out and I couldn't say no to his request for a one-on-one when Cass approached me with it.

Thank you, curious brain, you got me into the best kind of trouble tonight.

The minute our eyes locked on each other earlier, I knew our paths were meant to align. I could feel this instant unexplainable connection.

Maybe it was just sexual tension, but either way, I have never experienced anything like it, and the orgasm I had just from dry humping his cock was OUT OF THIS WORLD. Literally, I felt like I left the planet.

He may be around my age, but his dominance was such a turn on, and his words gahh… "It's Trent, so you can say it out loud when I make you come in a minute."

Not even sure how I responded to that, I just remember feeling desperate for him.

Pretty sure his next words put me over the edge, though.

"That's it… give it to me," he growled as he continued to drag my body over his lap, kissing all over my neck.

Feeling flushed, I pull up my mask to cool myself before I do something stupid—like run back into the room and beg him to fuck me.

Lost in thought, I almost get knocked over by someone walking down the hallway.

"Oh shit, are you o—Ashley? What the fuck?" Situating my mask, I look into a pair of familiar eyes…

Oh shit, is right.

My big brother drags me away, pissed as hell.

Pulling me into one of the secluded booths on the back of the main floor, he barks, "Ashley, start talking now!"

"Micah, I know what you're going to say, but you can save it." He's still fuming, so I continue.

"Don't you think I deserve a little freedom? I mean, come on, you know damn well my life is going to shit in a couple of years, so why the hell shouldn't I enjoy myself a bit?"

He's standing there, glaring at me with his arms crossed over his puffed-out chest. I place my hand on his shoulder to calm him.

"I know you don't understand because you get to do whatever you want, with whomever you want to do it with. You don't have this looming sense of doom always hanging over you."

I notice his hardened gaze soften. My brother may not be innocent in this life we live, but I know he loves me and wishes things were different.

"Ash, you know if I could change things, I would, but this is extremely dangerous. If Gio finds out you work here..." *He pauses for a moment to drag his hands over his face, steeping them over his mouth.* "You realize he's crazy enough to have you killed for something like this, right?"

I nod. "Yes, but honestly Mic, the way I see it, my life will be over soon either way, so I'm willing to take that chance." *I keep going because I know that's not what my brother wants to hear by the frown on his face.*

"I will say I chose this particular club as my bad girl rebellion because I know from an inside source that no one from the family is a member here. Speaking of which... What are you doing here?"

That turns his frown around. "That's true, Gio would have anyone's head that frequented this place instead of Sinners. And I'm meeting up with a close friend, so your secret is safe... for now." *He pauses, but I can tell he still has a point to make.* "However, that doesn't mean word couldn't get back to him from someone else. You know he has eyes everywhere."

He looks around at our surroundings to emphasize the fact that anyone could hear us. "I won't force your hand, but please consider doing something a little more discreet for your 'fuck everything' phase of life." *He lets out a long sigh.* "I currently have some things in the works. I'll get you out of this somehow. Have some faith, sis."

I love my brother dearly and I hope what he's saying is true, but in all reality, I must do what's best for me because the world we live in is a cruel one and can change in an instant.

I startle as a handful of popcorn hits my face.

"Are you even listening to me anymore?" I hear Lottie laugh out loud.

"Ugh, sorry," I mumble into my hands.

She lets out a sigh. "It's okay! I understand. Here I am blabbing about how incredibly delicious Greyson is, and I wasn't even thinking about what happened to you."

"Oh please, you should blab about how awesome your night was. You deserve it!" I give her the most serious look I can muster in my tipsy state. "Honestly Tig, I'm really fucking happy you had a great night."

She leaps across the bed like some sort of ninja and wraps her arms around me. She holds onto me for dear life. "Love you too, Bitty," she says into my chest. We stay like that for a moment while I pat her head.

Settling back into her spot across from me, she picks up her weird concoction of a snack. I stare at her as she munches away.

"Stop looking at me like that, it's so fricken good." She scoffs at me while throwing another handful into her mouth.

"Mm hmm, and supposedly so is butt sex, but you don't see me running to test it out."

She bursts into laughter. "What the fuck is wrong with you? How do you get anal from my popcorn and M&M mix? Your mind is permanently in the gutter."

I just raise my shoulders. I mean, she's not wrong. My mind is in the gutter ninety-nine percent of the time, but what nineteen-year-old's isn't?

"Please tell me what happened tonight… Maybe I can help in some way."

"Ugh… It's so damn surreal. I don't even know if it really happened."

She situates herself on the pillows and awaits patiently as I mentally sort through tonight's clusterfuck.

"Okay, so remember that guy back at Masqued from the beginning of the year?"

"Uhm, of course I do. You went over in explicit detail how hot that private dance was, and to my knowledge, it's the only one you've ever given."

I laugh. Yeah, I definitely gave her an exact play-by-play of that evening.

"Okay well, it's fucking him… the Joker is Trent from Masqued."

She looks at me, utterly shocked. "Shittt! You found this out at the beginning of the night or later on?"

"Ugh, don't judge my whorish ways! I didn't know his name until round two." I lay there, covering my face with my hands.

"Stahp! You didn't even ask his name before you guys had sex? What were you moaning… Joker?"

I raise an eyebrow. Does she really want me to answer that?

"Dayum girl, more power to ya. That's kinda hot though… What gave it away? I mean, it must've been hard to tell with his face paint tonight, and you said he was wearing a mask at the club." She takes a breath but continues to talk me through her entire thought process. "Oh, and I bet your blonde hair threw him off, too… But what about his voice? Didn't it sound familiar to you?"

"I mean, I kept getting a weird sense of familiarity all night and couldn't quite place it. The first night we met, we didn't exactly carry on a full-blown conversation. It was more like husky, lust-filled whispers."

"Okay, so how did you figure out it was Masqued Trent, then?"

"It just sort of happened... We were about to go for round two and he flipped me onto all fours. Then he whispered his name in my ear, took off my corset, saw my tattoo, and said, 'Maggie.'"

She gasps. "Holy Shit. You have got to be kidding me. What did you do?"

"I did nothing. Basically freaked the fuck out and ran. I think I said sorry, but I ran as fast as I could."

"Geez!" she lets out, but I can see her contemplating something.

"Out with it!" I tell her.

"Okay, so I get the fact that you freaked out, because what are the chances... but why is him being 'Masqued Trent' such a bad thing?" She looks at me as she continues, "Look, I know you're not looking for anything serious because of your situation, but wouldn't you rather have a steady hook up who knows that side of your life?"

I get what she's saying, but I feel like getting close to Trent would be dangerous, not only for him, but for me, too.

"I don't know... I'm leaving tomorrow. What difference would it make?"

Lottie gives me a knowing smile. "Well, you are coming back in a month, and you know damn well what happens at the beach stays at the beach."

"I like the way you think, Tig!"

We lay there quietly for a while, both reminiscing about our nights.

Maybe seeing him again wouldn't be the worst thing. The idea of being near him once more sets my body on fire. A big part of me wants to come back next month as planned, but tonight has me questioning everything.

This could be bad, very bad, but I can't seem to want to stop it.

Chapter Four

Trent

"Seriously Son, What the hell is going on with you lately? I have gotten used to dealing with your broody-ass cousin this summer, but where has my fun-spirited guy gone?"

I look up, shocked at my normally sweet mom, who is apparently calling my ass out.

"Sorry, I don't want to talk about it, but I'm fine. I'll snap out of it just for you, Mama. Wouldn't want you dealing with two assholes this summer," I say, trying to lighten things up.

She cracks a smile. "You better watch your mouth. Plus, I didn't say G was an asshole, he just isn't all sunshine and peaches either. I just want you to know I'm always here for you. No matter what, you can come to me."

I nod and give my saint-of-a-mother a quick peck on the cheek before going to the fridge for a snack as she retreats to her reading nook.

I certainly can't tell my mother that I'm still thinking about the best lay of my life with the most unbelievable chick and that she left me with no explanation.

Especially after fate put us back together. Yes, I said fate. I don't care how much of a pussy that makes me, but how else would you explain the hot little blonde bunny from last week turning out to be Maggie... *My Maggie* from the club whom I swear my dick still hasn't recovered from?

After Masqued, I kept telling myself she would've given me her number had it not been against the rules. I searched for her the rest of the night but never spotted her again, and Cass wouldn't give me any information.

So, I came back to North Carolina with my tail between my legs, knowing that I would probably never see the beauty again.

Honestly, when I saw her dancing in my living room, she was the first girl I'd truly wanted and felt drawn to since coming home from New York.

My ego took a big hit by her reaction when she found out it was me. So yeah, I've been moping around ever since.

Her best friend Lottie wouldn't give me any information other than she returned to NYC the day after the party.

I wanted to chase after Lottie as she ran out of the guest house because I knew she was going to my girl, but my pride wouldn't let me. She had already run out on me once, but dammit, I wanted some answers from her.

No one has ever affected me the way she has. I even got desperate enough to call my brother this week to see if he had seen her around the club. Trevor told me he hadn't, and that I needed to move on. He suggested I bury myself in one of my very willing fuck buddies to help take my mind off her.

I know he's right, but fuck, there's just something about her, and she's taking up way too much space in my head.

But today is looking up… I convinced Greyson to go with me to a friend's pool party. The plan to get shitfaced and forget my name and hopefully hers, too.

Three beers later and not nearly buzzed enough, I watch my cousin texting on his phone looking all happy and shit. I hate to be bitter, but it kinda pisses me off. I want my girl to text me. *My girl… fuck, I really am losing it.*

Instead, Felicity is sitting on my lap talking to her friend, who keeps rubbing my arm too. Clearly, they want to have some fun.

In the past, Felicity has been a good time, and we have let others join in on our fun a time or two. As hot as all that sounds, it's crazy how it doesn't even hold a candle to the time I've spent with Maggie.

Especially now that I've been inside her. I just can't seem to convince my dick that any other pussy could match up.

The girls keep eyeing G too, but he hasn't given them—or any other female—the time of day since he laid eyes on Lottie last weekend. He must have been feeling sorry for my ass since he agreed to come with me today.

Felicity flicks my arm, and it's then I realize she's asking me a question. "Think your cousin would want to join in? We could trade-off. Keep it interesting." I snort at her suggestion, seriously considering telling her to ask him herself, knowing damn well he would turn her down immediately, deflating the large ego she has developed over the years.

He doesn't exactly scream approachable since the only time he smiles is when he's texting with his girl.

I may have one inch on him in the height department, but he is a big, muscular mammoth of a guy. He isn't even eighteen yet and has a clean, cropped beard that would make men fifteen years his senior jealous. I am man enough to say the dude is good-looking... I mean, good genetics run in our family.

Speaking of the big guy, he gets up, not even acknowledging the girls. He looks at me and says, "I'm heading out, going to meet Lottie at the boardwalk."

I see that as my way out since I haven't had nearly enough to drink for my dick to agree to anything other than Maggie.

Tapping Felicity's leg, I nod for her to stand up. She looks at me with confusion as I turn my attention to G. "Okay, well, since I drove you here, I don't mind running you over there. I'm starving anyway."

Felicity pipes up, "What the fuck, Trent, you aren't staying to party? You know I have something here you can eat."

Not sure if she is being suggestive or not, but either way it's a no for me. "Yeah well, I have my mind on eating something in particular... something that isn't here." More like someone, but I'll leave that for her to interpret.

Jumping into my Jeep, G speaks up. "Damn, you are about as bad as me, turning down not just one pussy but two because they aren't the right one."

What the fuck is happening to me?

Well, if I was jealous of Greyson earlier, I am about to turn green right now watching him share a freaking ice cream cone with Lottie.

They have me thinking things I've never given two shits about, like how awesome a double date would be or a couple's trip. I have officially gone crazy. The girl I want to share a cone with as we walk along the boardwalk won't even talk to me.

Lottie must see my envy as she waves her hand for me to come over to where they are leaning against the pier rails.

"Trent, I'm going to take pity on you and tell you two things about Ashl… well, three things." A bit confused by the pause in her words, I look to her to go on because if it's about Maggie, I want to know it all.

She hands the ice cream cone to G and continues, "First off, her real name is Ashley. Maggie is the name she uses at the club. Yes, I know about you meeting her at the club, but that's all I'll say on that matter." Okay, her earlier pause makes sense now… Ashley… that suits her even more.

The fact she told Lottie about meeting me at the club gives me hope. I won't press her for more info since she is giving more than I thought she would, but man, I want to know if she told her about that night before last weekend or just after she figured out I was the Joker.

I nod for her to continue, still surprised she is opening up. "Second, she will be back in July to spend a week with me."

I can't help but smile. That makes the hope bloom even more with the chance of getting to see her again, but then a thought comes to mind. "Yeah, but she didn't seem like she wanted anything to do with me once she found out it was me, so how do I know she won't avoid me the whole time she's here? Or even worse, not show up at all."

That makes Lottie smile, and she says, "Remember, I am her very best friend, so if I'm telling you all this, there must be a reason, right? If I thought she didn't like you or truly didn't want to be around you, do you think I would even bother?"

Okay, that makes sense and makes me feel a hell of a lot better. "Fair point, so what's the last clue, Sherlock?" She smirks at me and gives me the universal sign for "hold please" as she pulls out her phone and starts clicking away.

I notice G is playing with her hair as she messes with her phone. Homie is already so wrapped around her finger, but I see why. These two chicks are unlike anyone I've ever seen, from their looks to the energy that surrounds them. Just something about them has drawn both of us southern boys in.

My phone chimes and I notice it's an Instagram notification. Lottie nods her head toward my phone. "Check it."

Opening it up, I see it's a follow request from a *LottieDee*. Before I can speak, she says, "Now add me back and peep my page. Your girl is all over it. I won't give you her number, and her account is private… so if she accepts your request and you happen to slide into her DMs, then that's on her."

I'm the happiest I've felt in a week. My fingers can't move fast enough to follow Lottie back and go right to her story where I see #nationalbestfriendday and the face of the most beautiful girl in the world fills my screen.

Seeing her in all these pictures reminds me of how much I want her. I can't wait a month until she visits again or take the chance of her not coming back this summer.

Chapter Five

Ashley

Mindlessly walking around the club tonight, I deliver drinks with a forced smile on my face. This used to be my haven… where I came to feel a little bit of control over my life, but now all it does is make me think of Trent and things that could never be.

I'm a stupid girl for holding on to the connection we have, but I just can't seem to let it go. Even more so now that I've been stalking his dangerously handsome face on Instagram. The summer sun has done nothing but make that man more enticing. Seeing photos of his tanned skin, perfectly tousled blonde hair, and drool-worthy eight pack had me eager to flirt with him via private message. All thanks to Lottie, of course.

Lottie posted a story the other day on the gram of her laying on her stomach on the beach with her perfect ass in all it's glory and right in the background were Trent and Greyson throwing a football. I have never felt any type of jealousy toward my best friend, but that day I couldn't help it.

What I would give to be on that beach gossiping with my bestie while we drool over our guys as they walk around shirtless. I sent a sad face emoji back in reaction to the story, then she cryptically asked me if I had checked my Instagram requests.

My curiosity was piqued, so I went right to my requests and saw one from Tmanning59. It was the third down on the list, but instantly caught my eye. Without giving it a second thought, I clicked confirm and immediately hit follow back.

My heart was going wild with anticipation... I can't explain the effect he has on me. I soon realized he'd sent me a message before accepting his request, so it was in a separate folder. I had to put my hand over my heart, willing it to calm down, and get my shit together.

My hands were shaky from nerves. Not knowing whether he was going to dig for answers as to why I ran away, or maybe he was going to curse me out from the blue balls I gave him when I left. But all my anxiety is relieved as soon as I open his message. Thankfully, he knows not to push me, even though he doesn't really know me at all.

> ***Tmanning59:*** *Hey Beautiful... I just wanted you to know I think Ashley suits you much better... and the blonde too.*
>
> ***Ashxox:*** *Oh yeah, well, I can't decide if Trent or Joker is a better fit for you. The jury's still out and thank you. :)*
>
> ***Ashxox:*** *P.S. Cute Bio... like how you threw in the fact you got a big dick but tried covering it up with your BDE: Boys Down East.*
>
> ***Tmanning59:*** *You lost me at "you got a big dick." Thank you and it's yours anytime you want it. :-)*
>
> ***Tmanning59:*** *But for real Boys Down East is a real thing. Go look up the hashtag smart ass!*
>
> ***Ashxox:*** *Hold please... runs to search #boysdowneast!*

Fucking A... he wasn't lying. So many pics of hot shirtless dudes at the beach, fishing, driving their boats, hanging out with other hot dudes, or should I say *Boys Down East*? There was even a pic of Trent standing on top of his Jeep on the beach that was posted by a Boys Down East fan page. These guys are like legends in North Carolina. I mean, they sure know how to breed them down there...

> ***Ashxox:*** *Okay, so you weren't lying... lots of good eye candy under that hashtag. Thanks for the plug :)*
>
> ***Tmanning59:*** *Watch it... I'll hunt you down and give you some eye candy all right.*
>
> ***Ashxox:*** *Pshhh whatever! Go tell that to one of your many fuck buddies.*

Okay, maybe I'm fishing here, but I can't help it. I know his type and I also know with his looks and many *talents,* he has them lining up at his door.

> ***Tmanning59:*** *See, that's the issue here, though. There is this one chick who is a mind-fuck and has now caused my dick to only want her, so it's not as easy as you make it sound. But... I have a plan!*

This guy is killing me. I'm seriously considering running away to North Carolina and begging him to move into a love shack on the beach with me.

I can't help but ask...

> ***Ashxox:*** *And what might that plan be, sir?*
>
> ***Tmanning59:*** *To make you miss me...*

Shit... What if I already do?

We continue to flirt via Instagram every day. Yesterday took a bit of a turn when he asked about me returning to Nori Beach in July. I was honest and told him I was still debating on if I was for sure coming or not. What I didn't tell him was that I just wasn't sure if I could handle being around him for an entire week.

Now that Lottie and his cousin Greyson are all hot and heavy, I know we would spend most of our time with them. I just don't know if I can stand only having Trent temporarily and giving him up when it's all said and done.

Even as a child, I never enjoyed playing with other people's things that I knew I could never have. If it wasn't something obtainable, I would rather not have a taste of it at all. The only problem is… I have had a taste of Trent, and I fucking loved every second of it.

Needless to say, with Trent on my mind constantly and the fact that I have felt this eerie feeling of being watched the last several days, I'm a bit on edge and not in the mood to be at work tonight.

I saw one of Gio's men in the coffee shop the other day watching me as I sipped my latte and read a book. I know for certain he wasn't there for the fresh brew.

It's just a matter of time before they crack down on me.

On top of that, I keep questioning if working here is worth the risk anymore. I originally started here as a cocktail waitress for the thrill of feeling fun and rebellious.

The job sort of just fell into my lap after getting an awesome opportunity through the owner of Masqued. Sloan, who is the coolest chick ever, owned and operated a popular sex blog before moving to New York and opening this club.

Sloan saw some of my designs at a competition my senior year and commissioned me to draw up some sketches to outfit her staff.

She invited me to the club to get some inspiration, and I immediately felt the thrill of being there. The anonymity coupled with the fun and rebelliousness was exactly what I needed. Before I left that day, I asked for a job.

In the beginning, working here was a lot of fun but lately, it's felt lackluster.

Snapping me out of my thoughts, Cass speaks up as she starts another round of drinks for my VIP table.

"Hey boo, why the long face? You've been distant all week. I miss that sparkly smile." Cass is like the big sister I never had. She is always looking out for me. She's the only person other than Lottie who knows about Trent and that I saw him again in North Carolina.

I give her a big smile. "Sorry. I know I've been in my shell a bit this week. But you're right. I need to smile more. The RBF isn't making me as many tips."

We both laugh before she places a round of Casamigos shots on my tray with limes and says, "Work that VIP section babe. With all the tequila they're drinking, they won't even care how much money they're giving you by the end of the night."

"I like how you think, Cass baby." I say as I sashay away towards the upper VIP lounge.

"Hi guys. Another round of shots… Are you celebrating something fun tonight?" I try to make small talk to make up for my standoffishness tonight. No one wants a sour puss for a cocktail waitress.

One guy speaks up, "As a matter of fact we are!" He points to his friend. "Our boy Jason turned thirty today!"

Looking over to where he's pointing, I find a very good-looking Jason smiling widely at me.

His loud friend speaks up again, "Would you be willing to do something for our birthday boy for us?"

Not liking where this is going, I frown slightly, but then pull myself back together and answer honestly. "Well, that depends on your request?"

Picking up the bowl of limes, he says, "Hold one of these in your mouth for our boy while he takes a shot. It will make the lime that much sweeter."

This dude is full of himself, but Jason doesn't seem so bad, and the request is tame compared to what I thought they were going to ask.

Grabbing a lime from the bowl as I shrug my shoulders, I say, "Sure, why not? Come on, Birthday boy." I hold the salted lime in the air and smile at Jason.

He stands up, grabbing a tequila shot. Wasting no time, he shoots it back then grabs me by the hips, pulling me towards him to suck on the lime.

I'm shocked when the sensual move elicits no reaction from me. Something about his touch is just not quite right, and maybe I'm more fucked than I thought. *Shit, this isn't good.*

Luckily, he is respectful, probably because he never has to beg for a woman's attention, and he gives me a wink. "Thanks for putting up with us and giving in to my friend's request."

"No problem. Happy Birthday!" Looking at the circle of guys, "Another round?"

A few of the guys cheer in unison, "Hell yeah!"

Approaching the bar again, I tell Cass I need six more shots and some help as I pretend to bang my head on the bar.

"What's wrong? Do I need to get security? Is someone in VIP being too handsy?" Her knee-jerk reaction has me laughing, but it makes sense in this line of work.

Shaking my head no, I tell her, "That's the issue. I gave him permission to touch me, but it did nothing for me. And he was freaking hot! What the fuck is wrong with me, Cass?"

Grabbing my arm across the bar for comfort, she says, "Babe, I think I know exactly what's wrong with you, or should I say who… Speaking of, his brother came by again the other night when you were off. He was asking about you for Trent."

I giggle. "That sounds like Trent. It's refreshing how persistent he is even after he already got the main thing most guys want. We've been messaging nonstop this week, and it has me questioning everything."

She grabs a rack of glasses along with a polishing cloth and says, "Sit! I'll have one of the other girls take this round to the VIP section. Polish these glasses while I give you my two cents."

I nod and reach for the cloth to get to work as she speaks again. "I know you have some demons that I don't know about, and I'm not asking you to tell them to me, but I do think life is too short to not go after what you want. It's okay to try something new. It may fail, it may go up in flames, but at least you know you tried instead of having regrets your whole life."

She pauses with a sad smile on her face before she continues, "Take it from someone a bit older than you that has made some choices in life I wish I could take back." She pauses and looks off as if recalling a distant memory.

Letting out a sigh, she continues, "I would give anything to go back and give in to those feelings just to see where things went. It was frowned upon by others in my life, so I let it slip away and now look at me. The judgmental people aren't in my life anymore, but neither is the one I truly wanted."

I know she's right, but she also doesn't know the extent of my issues. Unfortunately, mine puts lives at stake.

Smiling at Cass, hating that this wonderful blessing in my life isn't truly happy, I respond honestly. "Thanks for sharing that with me. Just your words alone have already helped me make one decision I was questioning regarding him."

"Good! I just want you to be happy, no matter what that means. I'm always here for you if you need me." The machine spits out another slip. That draws Cass' attention back to the bar.

"I better get back to work. Finish those glasses for me pretty please, and then go make that money, honey!"

"Sure thing." I speak up again before she walks away. "Cass… I feel it in my bones. Your happiness isn't far away. You're too amazing not to have it all." She blows me a kiss and smiles as she heads back to the bar.

One thing that is clear after hearing her talk is I am for sure going back to the beach this summer. I've already come to terms with giving up my dreams of a fairytale love story and a future as an elite designer… but nothing is saying I have to give up my week at the beach. I'm giving myself that. Besides, it's only one week.

A week in Nori Beach, my happy place, with not only my best friend but also the hottest guy on the planet. This is going to be epic.

My mood has drastically improved, and I've never enjoyed polishing glasses so much in my life. That is until my mind wanders and I recall Gio's guy in the coffee shop. I have to start being more careful on my commute to work and be more aware of my surroundings. I've been careless in that sense.

Suddenly, I feel electrified, like the buzz you get from a pre-workout... where the hell did that come from? It's like the energy in the room has changed, but not in an eerie way like the feeling I was having earlier. No, this is different. Only one person has made me feel this way before.

I can feel the hair on the back of my neck rise. A warm tingle shoots to my toes as a familiar husky voice comes from behind, whispering in my ear, "Miss me yet?"

Chapter Six

Trent

Sitting in the run-down diner, I can't help but feel anxious as the elevated train runs by, shaking the walls of the place. Shit, I hope it doesn't collapse. Considering the severely worn red leather booths are mostly held together by tape, it doesn't look like it would take much for it to fall apart. The smoke-stained walls and shelves are decorated with forties and fifties memorabilia, which seem to be more from lack of updating than nostalgia.

The hostess, Fran, was quite welcoming. She's a much older woman with the deep voice of a long-time smoker. She called me sweetheart one too many times during our brief interaction, but sat me in the far corner as I requested.

I guess this place really doesn't give a shit whom it serves alcohol to because when I asked for a beer, she barely glanced at my fake ID and returned quickly with my drink. At least it has that going for it.

Fuck, man, Ashley didn't appear as happy to see me as I would have hoped. Her face did light up immediately, but it was short-lived and disappeared in an instant. She was so quick to dismiss me and get me out of there. In fact, she seemed really on edge.

Is she seeing someone else? Did I misjudge our DMs?

Running my hands over my face, I let out a frustrated growl. I'm such a fucking idiot. This is not me. I don't fawn over girls like this. They come to me. I don't chase them... They chase me. But for some reason, I'm sitting here—alone—waiting for her like she asked me to.

What am I even doing here? I grab my wallet and throw down a twenty-dollar bill. I finish my beer by chugging it, then stand to leave.

"Shit, don't leave." I hear coming from the left of me.

Looking up, I lock on to the most gorgeous set of blue eyes. My body instantly relaxes at the sight of her.

She's here.

Dammit, I'm like a fucking puppy dog, all excited because Ashley actually showed up.

Shit, why did I admit that... man-the-fuck-up, Trent.

"Why wouldn't I?" She looks confused by my response, so I clarify. "Didn't really receive the reaction I was expecting when I showed up."

"Shit Trent, I'm sorry." She looks up at the ceiling as if trying to keep herself from tearing up.

"I've been on edge all night. Then you showed up, and I was so distracted that I didn't get to give you the warm welcome you deserved."

Ashley leans in and lightly brushes her lips over mine. It's sweet and all, but certainly not enough to feed the hunger that has built up inside of me. I grab her by the back of her neck and deepen our kiss. I swipe my tongue across her lips, demanding they open.

Her body responds immediately by pressing into mine. She opens her sweet mouth and moans as our tongues collide.

I forget we're not alone for a few moments, only brought back to reality when I hear Fran's gruff voice from across the diner. "All right, Casanova, cut that shit out."

I feel Ashley's lips smile as she takes my hand, and we sit back down in the booth.

I'm hard as a motherfucker. Once we sit, she catches me adjusting myself and smirks at me.

"I wouldn't be laughing, Doll. You're going to be helping with this situation by the end of the night."

"Oh! Is that so, Mr. J?" She laughs just as Fran approaches our table.

"What can I get you two lovebirds besides a room?" she asks in that thick New York accent of hers.

"I'll have another beer." Looking over at Ashley, I give her a nod for her to order.

"I'll have a water, please. Oh, and a double cheeseburger plus a large cheese fry... hmm, and also a black and white milkshake with whipped cream."

The look on Frans's face is comical considering this bombshell next to me just ordered enough food for a man my size.

"All right, I'll be back soon," Fran says as she walks away.

Ashley turns her body so it's facing mine in the booth. I take in the sight of her.

Her face is washed clean from the makeup she wears to work, although her lips are swollen from the fuck-hot kiss we shared just moments ago. Her blonde hair is piled into a bun on top of her head and she's in a pair of ripped jeans and an oversized t-shirt. I don't think she has ever looked more gorgeous than she does at this very moment.

She catches me staring and smiles. *Fuck, I'm in trouble.*

"Was this your plan all along? Surprise me in New York."

I can't tell her it's because I'm basically obsessed with her and want to make sure she isn't going to back out of coming to Nori Beach again in a couple of weeks.

"Not exactly…" I stop mid-sentence when I see Fran approaching with our drinks. I don't think Fran's ears could handle what I really had planned for Ashley this weekend.

"Here you go sweethearts, food will be out shortly." We thank her as she walks away.

Staring at Ashley as she puts her lips to her straw, has me wanting to see her perfectly plump lips wrapped around my cock. In fact, I'm fucking aching to have her again.

"So…" I start, hoping like hell she will give me some insight as to why the fuck she left me the way she did.

"Sooo…" she replies with a smile.

I don't like games, and I certainly don't like the runaround. Is she really not going to explain what the fuck happened that night?

I guess if she wants to ignore it, then we will… I will just make sure to tie her up this time so she can't run out after our first round.

"I got a hotel room for the weekend… I'm in New York till Monday morning. I was hoping you'd spend some time with me."

I see the hesitation on her face before she even opens her mouth to speak.

"I don't know, Trent… I'm not sure that's the best idea." She almost looks sad when she says it.

I raise a brow and just look at her, hoping she'll elaborate.

She lets out a deep sigh. "I would love nothing more than to be locked up in a hotel room with you all weekend."

I feel the but coming…

"But I just don't think it's a good idea. I already enjoy my time with you too much and I know I can't have more." She looks down at her intertwined fingers. "I have future family obligations and they leave me no room to have a life outside of it. If we continue this, it will only be that much harder when that time comes."

I nod in response, unable to find the right words.

Is that why she ran out? I won't push her for those answers, at least not just yet. I can tell this upsets her. What the hell could it be?

Thankfully, Fran arrives with the food to help ease the awkwardness at the table.

We stay quiet for a few moments while she snacks on the fries and takes some big sips from her milkshake.

She moans, "Holy shit, this has got to be the best tasting milkshake."

"Really? I highly doubt that. What the hell is a black and white shake, anyway?"

"Shut up! You've never heard of a black and white. It's literally the best thing ever… It's vanilla ice cream with chocolate syrup."

I quirk my eyebrow. "Isn't that the same as using a scoop of chocolate and a scoop of vanilla to make it?"

"Nope! Absolutely not. It can *only* be made this way." She laughs as she takes another long pull from the drink.

"You have got to try it," she adds as she shoves the straw at me.

I take a long pull but get distracted by her tongue that sneaks out of her mouth to clean the shake from her lips. I'm instantly hard again.

She's watching me intently and I remember she's awaiting the results of my taste test.

"It's good, I guess," I say with a shrug. I'm lying, this shit is delicious, but I want to mess with her a bit. "It wouldn't be my first pick. I'm more of a cookies and cream type of guy."

Ashley stares at me, baffled. "That's it. Now I'm certain we could never work out."

We both crack up laughing. She's so damn beautiful when she smiles.

I need to figure out a way to make this work.

I find myself just sitting there smiling at her, so happy to be here in this moment.

"What are you smiling at?" she asks while self-consciously wiping at her mouth.

"You… I'm staring at your gorgeous smile and wondering what makes you tick. Tell me something about yourself."

"Uhm… geez, I don't know. I like to sew in my spare time."

"Interesting. I wouldn't have pegged you as a sewer, no offense, but that's my grandma's hobby too," I say as I reach across to grab a fry, but one hits me in the face before I reach it.

"Do not compare me to your grandma if you know what's best for you." We both laugh and she continues, "No, really, I love designing and creating pieces. It's my dream job, actually."

Ashley lets out a large sigh. I let her bask in her thoughts for a moment while I take another large sip of her milkshake.

That thing is so damn good.

She smirks when I push the glass back in front of her.

"I also love to hike. Growing up, my parents used to plan our family vacations around spots my brother and I could explore. Gives you such a sense of freedom when you get to the top of the mountain."

"Remind me to take you to the lookout next time you're in Nori Beach. It's awesome up there and you get the most amazing view of the boardwalk and the coast." I tell her, also trying to bait her to see if her plans are still on for July.

"I'd love that," she responds with a soft smile.

"What about you? Tell me something about yourself."

"Hmm… I took gymnastics and dance lessons for about seven years."

"Stahp really?" The wide grin that's plastered on her face sets my soul on fire and I'd do just about anything to keep it there.

"Swear! So did most of my football team growing up. It helps a ton with our agility on the field, even some famous NFL players take dance."

"Hmm, now I see where you got those dance moves from," Ashley says, while popping another fry into her mouth.

"Okay, my turn… What's your favorite childhood memory?" I ask.

"Hmm, I would say cooking with my grandma. We were always together in the kitchen growing up. I think I was making Sunday sauce by myself by the time I was ten. To this day, I don't think I have found a restaurant that could outshine her cooking.

"She was also an amazing baker. Gah… she used to make the best pignoli cookies from scratch. Around the holidays it was like a bakery exploded in her house, so many delicious treats from one end to another."

"So, what you're saying is… I shall be expecting a home-cooked Sunday dinner soon?" I joke with her.

Winking back, she replies, "Sure thing hotshot." She pauses, then asks, "Okay, what about you? What was your favorite memory growing up?"

I pause to think for a moment while taking another pull from the milkshake straw.

"I would say camping on the beach with Greyson as a kid. The beach starts not too far from the end of my property, so we would trek across my yard and through a small, wooded area and set up camp there. We'd pack up our wagon with all the essentials that a nine- and ten-year-old thought were needed to survive overnight… So clearly nothing helpful." I let out a laugh, recalling those nights.

"I remember this one time we forgot our snacks back at the house and we both refused to go get them. I didn't want to go back because it was G's fault we didn't have them. He didn't want to go because he said it was my fault, so clearly neither of us went back, refusing to admit responsibility. We were so fucking hungry, too. My mom must have known and right before she went to bed that night, she showed up with our packed cooler of snacks. Said she was waiting to see if we would cave, but couldn't bear to let us starve to death, either."

"That sounds amazing. I could just picture the two of you with your backpacks and flashlights venturing out and fending for yourselves."

"Yeah, those were the days."

We continue asking each other questions and getting to know one another for what seems like only a short while. It isn't until Fran drops off our check that I realize it's almost two a.m.

Not wanting this night to end, I try to convince her to come back with me. "What would you say if I asked you again to come back to the hotel with me tonight?"

She goes to reply, but I quickly blurt out, "We don't even have to do anything besides talk. I'm really enjoying getting to know you."

Ashley quirks her eyebrow at me, as if questioning my intentions.

"Okay, not going to lie. I would love to touch you. In fact, I would love to tie you to my bed and never let you leave. Making you come undone beneath me until the sun comes up. But... if all you want is to talk, I'll take that too."

Her gaze drops to her hands again.

Shit.

"Listen, you don't have to say anything. I get it, well, sort of… It is what it is. If you change your mind, I'm in room 525." I slide the extra key card across the table.

She's still quiet beside me. So, I decide I need to man up and accept our fate.

This shit sucks.

I throw down enough cash to cover our check and a tip for Fran. I kiss her on the cheek and stand to leave.

"I had a great time with you tonight, Ash. I hope you change your mind… about everything."

She finally looks up at me with glassy eyes. "I wish I could, more than you know."

"Goodbye, Doll," I say and leave the diner.

I don't look back, unwilling to see the tears I know are cascading down her cheeks.

This can't be over, not yet at least.

Ashley

I am a complete train wreck of emotions right now. From feeling such relief after talking with Cass to utter excitement when I felt Trent's touch. Then to complete terror when I recognized two of Gio's men walking to a table on the main floor of Masqued while Trent's arms were wrapped around me.

Ugh! Not to mention the absolute war in my head over whether I should take Trent up on his offer, especially after getting to know him more at the diner.

See... I, Ashley Castrovinci, am a TOTAL fucking disaster right now!

I felt terrible rushing Trent out of Masqued and then making him wait so long for me at the diner, knowing he came all this way to surprise me. But once I saw Gio's men, I was more concerned about our safety. Leaving the club right after him, I took the long route to the diner just in case anyone was trailing me.

The men that were there aren't the guys I've seen following me in the past, so it could have just been a coincidence. Regardless, I wasn't taking any chances.

Getting to know Trent tonight just made things that much harder. Seeing those sexy green eyes in person had me wanting so badly to throw caution to the wind.

Coming home to an empty house doesn't help with my wandering thoughts. My parents are on one of their many lavish weekends away, and my brother has his own place now. He hasn't lived here in quite some time, but his absence is still felt.

I know my family all love me and empathize with me, but none of them truly understand my feelings. They think I'm blowing this shit out of proportion, which I'm not. I just wish we didn't live under such archaic rules.

My brother says he's sorry for the shit hand I've been dealt, but does he even really get it? I mean, at the end of the day, he still gets to do whatever the fuck he wants because he is a man and that's all that matters in the world we live in.

Then you have my parents who got about as lucky as any made man and Italian princess can be. They had an arranged marriage, but they fell deeply in love with each other. Which is extremely rare under the circumstances.

My father often likes to remind me of that and to keep an open mind regarding my inevitable future.

3 YEARS EARLIER

I'm sobbing into my mother's chest, begging her to fix this as she rubs my hair silently. Not saying a word, just trying to soothe me and help me process the bomb they just dropped on me.

I hear my father's voice, soft but stern, "Isabelle, leave us please. I want to talk to my princess."

Looking up at him with more disdain than I ever have before, I say, "DO NOT call me that. If I was your princess, you would not be making me do this!"

As one of the most trusted soldiers in the Santini crime family, my father doesn't take disrespect lightly, but right now, he knows I have every right to be upset. My whole life has been turned upside down. One moment I'm a normal teenager living my life and the next I'm being informed of my wedding date to a complete stranger.

He takes my mother's place beside me, but I don't give him a chance to speak before I tell him exactly how I feel.

"This is such bullshit. I was always made to believe that because of your position in the family, I wouldn't have my husband chosen for me. Now suddenly, I am being promised to the worst of the worst. Giovanni Junior!"

My father decides to speak up then. "You don't even know Junior."

"I know of the stories of his father, who is as unpredictable as he is malicious. Per your mouth."

"His son has a better head on his shoulders. Our families are seeing eye to eye more than ever, with Junior taking over some of the control. I believe he will treat you well and you could have a great life with him. Look at your mother and me. I met her for the first time three months before we were married, and it was love at first sight. She is my everything."

I pull on my hair, wanting to pull it out as I growl at my father. "And you know that is a rarity. Name one other couple we associate with who has the type of love you and mom share. Name one other made man who has stayed faithful to his wife and kids?"

My father's silence is an answer in itself. I may only be sixteen, but I'm mature for my age and always pay attention when it matters, as he has taught me.

"Why me?" I sob again, thinking about my dreams of a fairytale love story I'd always hoped I would have one day.

My father lightly strokes my hair, trying to calm me down. "Sweetheart, as you know I'm one of Santini's most trusted men, and I have moved up in the ranks over the years, which makes me and my family more involved." Pointing from himself to me, insinuating my involvement just because I'm his daughter.

Continuing, he says, "At the black and white gala last month, you stunned Gio and his people when they saw you all grown up. Your beauty was expected because it was often said you were the spitting image of your mother, who is always the most gorgeous woman in the room. Well, at the Gala, you gave her a run for her money and since you are single and unpromised, a buzz started and hasn't stopped until this morning when we made it official."

He pauses and I don't even know what to say. Maybe I should be flattered, but I can't find it in me to feel anything other than dread and anxiety regarding my future. My dreams of a career in fashion design and of a loving family are now totally out of my control, and that's freaking scary to me.

Now that I've stopped crying again, my father must take that as a sign that I've accepted my fate. He stands but leans down to kiss the top of my head and says, "Ash, I would never allow harm to be brought upon you. I expect Junior to treat you with love and respect or else he will have to answer to the Santinis because this binding is helping them as well. Therefore, you will be under their protection."

He lifts my chin so I'm looking at him. "Just give him a chance, princess. He may surprise you."

I give my father a nod, but inside my wheels are turning and I'm already thinking of a way out of this. I refuse to live a life I don't want to live.

The memory of that conversation does absolutely nothing to ease my thoughts. Deciding I can't sit in this house any longer, I grab my key chain that has a full can of pepper spray attached and head out into the warm summer night for a walk.

Even at night, the mugginess that summer always brings to the city hits me when I step out of our brownstone. It's nothing like a summer night's walk on the beach in North Carolina. Not much can compare to that. Especially if it involves a certain local hottie who makes my knees weak.

See, this is what my life has turned into. I can't even think about the New York City heat without my thoughts venturing back to him. I don't know if it's the fact that I can't truly have him that's making him even more irresistible to me, or if it's just him. Honestly, I think it's the latter.

As I wander around the city, not knowing where exactly I'm going, I let my thoughts turn to Trent.

From the first moment we laid eyes on each other, there has just been something unexplainable about him. Even at the party in Nori Beach, I felt the pull toward him.

I love to have a good time and am by no means innocent, but I normally make them work a little harder before I get taken against a guy's bedroom wall. But with him, I knew within a few minutes of dancing that I had to have him, and fast.

Now that I've had him, the need is even worse. The way he continues to not give up on me is such a turn on and it's fucking with my head. The main problem isn't him, it's me. I'm scared I'll want more from him than just being his fuck buddy, and I know that can't happen.

Then, on the other hand, can't I just let myself have fun with him? At least in Nori Beach, I wouldn't have to worry about any watchful eyes. I'm not important enough yet for Gio to have me followed out of state.

As long as we're both on the same page about what this can and can't be, then maybe it can work. Right?

I hope for my heart's sake it can.

One thing I know for certain is that next month's beach trip to see my bestie will most likely be my favorite one yet.

Chapter Seven

Trent

Who the fuck is knocking on my door at three in the morning? I mute the TV and lay there, hoping it's just someone too drunk to function, trying to find their room.

Shit, I wish I was in the same inebriated state, too. Maybe my mind wouldn't be so torn up right now. Then I hear the light knocking once more.

Throwing the blankets off my lap, I hope whoever's on the other side is ready to get their ass handed to them. I'm in no mood to be fucked with. I know I've been a moody piece of shit the last two weeks, but right now there's no telling what I'm capable of.

Still can't believe she let me leave the diner without so much as an explanation. At this point, I don't even need answers, I just need her. I thought I had her for a moment there. The way Ashley looked at me when she asked me to stay.

Fuck man, I would give her anything she could ever dream of if she promised to always look at me like that. Like I was the answer to all her questions, to all her fears and doubts.

Let's not forget about the way she kissed me. That kiss was... that kiss was everything. It told me more about how Ashley was feeling than words ever could. I just need to stop thinking about it... it's over. *Over before it even truly began.*

I'm so fucked in the head. I look at myself in the mirror, pausing momentarily to take a look at the pathetic man in the reflection. *What has she done to me?*

I march my ass to the door and yank it open with more force than necessary.

"What do..." I stop immediately, the words getting stuck in my throat.

She's here. Blue eyes pleading with mine.

I close my eyes and let out a long breath. My Ashley's here.

Before I know what hits me, I'm being pounced on by the beautiful girl I thought I lost for good.

She wraps her legs around my waist, and I eagerly grab hold of her deliciously thick ass to help support her. Her lips smash into mine, her tongue quickly finding its way into my mouth with hunger. I feel like I can finally breathe again.

With her body securely attached to mine, I turn and kick the door closed behind us.

She breaks away from our kiss and smirks. "I'm glad you were awake."

"So am I, Doll, so am I." I kiss her neck, taking full advantage of our position. I nip and lick her from her ear to her collarbone, making her moan and grind down on my cock.

Making our way across the room, I smile as an ingenious plan crosses my mind.

"Why do you have such a devilish look in your eye right now?" Ashley says as I sit her down on the bed.

"Take off your clothes, lay back, and you'll find out."

She quickly shimmies out of the clothes she's wearing and crawls to the top of the bed.

I move her around a bit to get her into the perfect position. "Stay here and close your eyes for me."

"Should I be worried?" She giggles from her position on the bed, closing her eyes like I told her to.

"Oh, you'll see," I say over my shoulder as I walk towards the hotel room closet. I search around, collecting the necessary objects, and head back towards her, grabbing the ice bucket on my way.

Placing the items down on the bedside table, I pause to run my fingertip over her naked body. Her chest is rising and falling quickly, and I know my girl is wet for me.

My cock is aching to be inside of her, but I need to draw this out. I'm going to take my time and make her realize what she almost let walk away.

I make quick with my preparations and then grab her right arm and attach the belt of the hotel robe with a slipknot around her delicate wrist. She gasps in surprise and squeezes her eyes shut.

That earns her a kiss on her cheek, "Good girl. Keep those eyes shut."

Ashley wiggles her body in anticipation but keeps her eyes closed like I asked.

Walking around to the other side, I repeat the same slip knot to her left wrist. She lightly pulls on the makeshift restraints and smiles.

Making my way back over to the side table, I pull out the bottle of champagne I had ordered prematurely when I had thought Ashley would come back with me. I untie the thick ribbon from the bottle's neck and drape it over her eyes.

She's so quiet. I wonder what she is thinking right now. Is she going crazy with a need so strong it hurts to think about it? The same need that has consumed me since the moment our eyes met.

I can't wait to sink deep inside of her. Fucking her till I've had my fill. The only problem is I don't know if I ever will.

"Tilt your head to the left for me, Doll." She does as she's told once more, and I can't help but smile. Oh, this is going to be fun.

I tie the ribbon, move her head, and fix the pillow under her.

She moans in anticipation, writhing in the bed before me.

Fucking beautiful.

Leaning over her, I pause just above her lips, waiting to see if she'll push up to meet mine. Does she want this as bad as I do? She's here, isn't she?

A moment later, she lifts her head ever so slowly and lightly brushes her lips across mine.

I deepen our kiss until I steal the breath from her lungs, until she realizes that this is where she's supposed to be.

Breaking away, I kiss my way down her front. Kissing a trail down her body until I'm looking up at Ashley from between her legs.

I drag my tongue along the inside of her thigh, making her squirm under me. I tease her folds but don't make contact with her delicious center yet.

She's going to have to wait it out. I'm going to tease the shit out of her first. Make her pay for teasing me, playing with my head like that.

I lick up the other thigh, torturously slow.

"Fuck…" she groans. "Stop teasing me!"

"Oh baby girl, you have no idea what I'm going to do to you tonight." With that, I sit up abruptly and get off the bed.

"Wait… Where are you going?" she blurts quickly.

"Don't you worry, I'm right here." I grab a piece of ice from the ice bucket and kneel next to her on the bed.

Holding my closed fist above her naked body, I let the ice melt from the warmth of my palm. Letting a few drops of water trickle onto her body, she yelps and twists her body when the droplets touch her flesh.

I continue torturing her for a few moments, keeping her guessing about its next location.

Discarding the ice chip, I grab another, except this time I place it in my mouth. Holding the piece between my teeth, I kiss her collarbone. The heat from my mouth makes her body melt beneath me. Then when the ice chip contacts her skin, she stiffens, gasping from the contact.

I travel down her body at an agonizingly slow pace, stopping at her hardened nipples. My mouth is on them instantly. Tonguing the bud with my icy cold mouth. The sensation of my chilled lips and hot tongue seem to be driving her crazy by the way she is moaning and grinding into my mouth.

Ashley yanks on her restraints, and her chest rises off the mattress. "Shit! Holy shit… ahhh. You have to stop. I can't take it anymore!"

I smirk at her as I sit back on my knees, giving myself a firm tug readjusting my throbbing cock.

Damn, she's so fucking perfect.

Lying there with a gorgeous blush on her skin, her pouty mouth agape and panting. Ashley's long blonde hair fans out over my pillow, and I can't wait to wrap it around my hand later. Her toned body wriggles before me as she rubs her thighs together, trying to relieve the tension I know is thrumming through her.

Something comes over me at the thought of having her tied up, her body begging me to touch it. I did this to her.

Spreading her legs, I drag my finger up her pussy. She moans at my touch. "You like that Doll?"

"Oh, please yes!" she groans as I do it again.

Placing another piece of ice in my mouth, I situate myself between her thighs.

This time I won't avoid her aching pussy. I dive right the fuck in.

After all, I am a starved man.

"Holy shit, Trent!" Ashley groans, tugging on the restraints, trying to reach my head.

I lick and flick my tongue along with the ice cube all over her sex. She squirms beneath me.

Fuck, she's delicious.

Her guttural moans spur me on, and I am overcome with need. I need to fill this perfect pussy of hers and feel her clench around me.

But first, my girl needs to come. I think I've tortured her enough. Coating my fingers in her sweet juices, I push in two achingly slow. Her back arches off the bed.

"Yes, that's right... Are you ready to come for me, Doll?" I practically growl from between her legs.

"Oh fuck... Yes, please!" she begs.

I dive back in, humming my appreciation for her submission. I can tell Ashley enjoys being in control in most aspects of her life. She's a strong-willed, take-no-shit type of woman, coupled with the fact that I have her in such a vulnerable position and she's accepting it... I can't think of anything sexier than that.

Her legs begin to tighten on me, and I feel her pussy pulse around my fingers. I suck on her clit one last time, igniting a fire that rips through her body. She lets out such a euphoric sound that I have to grab my cock to calm myself the fuck down.

Her body convulses under my touch and I'm smug as fuck. I did this to her. This beautiful creature is mewling for me.

I can't take it anymore and I climb up her body. Reaching over, I grab a condom and sheath my aching cock as quickly as possible. I don't give her any time to recover before I'm pushing inside.

"Holy shit," she screams when I thrust my hips, filling her completely with each stroke.

We fall into a steady rhythm, and she rocks her hips in sync with each of my thrusts.

"That's it, baby, ride my cock... Fuck, your pussy is unreal."

"My god you feel so good. Please don't stop," she begs as she tries to maneuver her hands to my shoulders and fails because of her restraints.

But I need to feel her hands on me.

Holding still momentarily so I can take off her blindfold and untie her wrists, once free, her hands immediately reach for me like she was dying for this connection as well.

Lifting one of her legs over my shoulder, I continue to rock my hips into hers.

She moans in pleasure when my hand reaches her clit. Rubbing it slowly, I can feel her body climbing once more.

"Yes, that's it… give it to me." I thrust harder into her as her body trembles.

"Good girl." At that, she screams out her release. Her head drops back, and her eyes roll as the orgasm takes over.

Fuck, she's squeezing me so damn tight I can't hold on much longer. Two more thrusts and I follow with my own.

When the last of my cum fills the condom, I groan. I wish there was nothing between us. I want to feel her milk my cock dry with no barriers.

Collapsing onto my elbows, I kiss her panting mouth. Her tongue dives into mine.

We kiss like this is the start of something new between us. Like she's finally agreeing that she needs this as much as I do.

That makes me so happy.

"You made my night," I blurt out as I stare at her beautiful face below me.

She smiles coyly. "I'm glad I came."

I kiss her softly as I pull out of her and head to the bathroom, needing to dispose of the condom.

I smile to myself in the bathroom mirror. *She's here.*

The darkness outside my hotel window is fading as dusk approaches.

Pulling back the covers, Ashley climbs into bed. I situate myself behind her and wrap my arms around her naked body. She feels so fucking good in my arms. I never want this feeling to end.

"Listen, Trent, I want to…" she begins before I hold my finger to her lips, silencing her. I don't want to hear the 'we can't do this' right now. I just want to soak up this moment with her.

"Shh, it's okay Ash. We can figure it all out tomorrow. Right now, I just want to enjoy having you here in my bed."

"Okay." She turns her head and kisses me deeply, then rolls back onto her side.

"Good night, baby," I say as I kiss her shoulder, hugging her tightly against me.

"Good night, T." She yawns as she wriggles her body to fit into mine.

I fall asleep with her securely in my arms and a smile on my face.

Fucking perfect.

I wake up to the sun blaring in my eyes and a cold pillow beside me. Before I have time to flip out that she left again, I spot a ripped piece of paper on the bedside table.

I'm sorry I had to go—
I'll see you in Nori Beach in 2 weeks!
xox, Ash
(212) 908-4065

Chapter Eight

Ashley

I have never been so freaking nervous in my life.

My best girl picked me up from the airport late last night. In true Tig and Bitty fashion, we stayed up all night binging unhealthy shit and talking about two hot-as-fuck cousins. The more the edible kicked in, the weirder the snacks and convos became.

Somehow, we dragged our asses out of bed and made it to the beach this morning. There's nothing like taking a nap under the warmth of the sun on a breezy afternoon.

It was such a beautiful, relaxing Monday. I love how Nori Beach always makes me slow down and enjoy the moment.

But now my nerves have no chill because Lottie and I are on the way to Trent and Greyson's where, and I quote, "We are supplying the takeout, movies, and orgasms. Y'all just bring your pretty asses over here."

I've lived for his text messages over the past two weeks… especially the filthy ones. He's such a dirty talker. Gah, it's so hot.

Lottie must've caught me smiling to myself and swats me on the arm.

"What?" I question.

"Girl, stop fantasizing about Trent. You'll be riding his dick soon enough!" She laughs out loud.

"I'm not going to jump him as soon as I see him. I do have some self-control, ya know."

"Mm hmm, whatever you say." She smiles, keeping her eyes on the road.

Grinning to myself once again because I really don't know if I'm going to be able to stop myself tonight.

Just thinking about him has me all worked up. The way he makes me laugh, his smile, and the way he works my body like he controls it. To be honest, just his words alone get me going now. He's literally like a walking wet dream.

> **BDE**
> Since you're the co-star in all of my fantasies these days, want to know one of my favorites?

> **ME**
> oOoOO do tell??

> **BDE**
> You know the back hallway at Masqued... The first place I got to see you cum for me?

> **ME**
> Of course, how could I forget?

> **ME**
> Come on, give it to me... what happens in the back hallway in this fantasy?

BDE
Oh, I'll give it to you all right baby girl:)

BDE
When I was walking down the hall to get a private show from the girl of my dreams, a chick named Maggie... know her???

ME
Middle Finger Emoji... too soon.

BDE
Sorry I couldn't resist

BDE
Anyways, I saw this big dude getting head in one of the rooms. I paid little attention to it at the time because I was anticipating the show I was about to experience from you. But ever since that night... I have jacked off so many times to thoughts of you blowing me in one of those rooms while whoever wants to can walk by and see the hottest girl on planet earth choking on my dick.

ME
The "choking on my dick" part has me way too eager now. Tell me more...

BDE
First off, you'd have that pretty little mask on so all I can see when I look at your face are those damn eyes that make me crazy and your plump lips wrapped around my fat cock. I want you wearing that little black dress you were wearing the first night I saw you, too. That way I can see your hard nipples easily with no one else getting a glimpse.

BDE
Are you touching yourself? I'm already stroking my dick just thinking about it. I would have to control myself from fucking your face... I mean, unless you like that.

> **ME**
> Yes, I am... and if you keep this up, I am going to have to put my phone to the side so my vibrator can finish the job.

> **ME**
> Second, you don't have to control yourself with me. I can take it... let's just say I have a special set of skills you haven't experienced yet.

> **BDE**
> Fuck yes, Doll. I am literally leaking for you. Please tell me you'll show me that special skill set next week??

> **ME**
> I plan on it. I'm ready to get on my knees for you, T.

> **ME**
> One more question before I go... take care of things. Would you fuck me in that room for others to see too?

> **BDE**
> Only with the privacy mode on the door. Seeing your mouth is one thing, but when you are with me... that pussy is MINE and no one else gets to see that or those perfect tits of yours.

> **ME**
> Shit... Why does that turn me on even more?

> **BDE**
> Because even though you may not be able to, your pussy wants to be MINE.

That whole text thread was so freaking hot, but again the feeling of fear got to me once I came down from my orgasm. The fear wasn't from his possessiveness itself, but by how much him calling me HIS felt so right.

Putting the car in park, Lottie looks over at me. "Why are you so nervous? From what you told me, you guys had a great time together in New York, and no one is trailing you here… Did something else happen you didn't tell me about?"

Shaking my head, I say, "No, I'm just scared." It comes out like a whisper, even though I don't mean it to.

My best friend pulls me into a hug across the center console. "I am so sorry for the cards you've been dealt. I can't imagine how hard it is, but just try to enjoy yourself and make the most of every moment of freedom you have."

I kiss her on the cheek, pulling back slightly to give her a big smile. "Thanks, Tig, I'm not worried about enjoying myself. I'm worried about enjoying myself too much. I just need to keep my feelings in check, and it'll be all good."

I know my body will be happy with me even if my heart and soul take a beating.

She nods while opening her door. "Okay boo, let's do this. I know two guys who will certainly be excited to see us."

Trent

"Seriously, man, you need to chill the fuck out," G says to me from the other side of the kitchen. I'm calm. I mean, I'm not going crazy or anything, just anxious. I can't wait to wrap her in my arms and devour that delicious mouth of hers.

Like he's one to talk anyway, he's busy polishing the damn refrigerator for fuck's sake. He has literally spent the entire day cleaning. Ha! And he says I'm the nervous one.

"Whatever G, finish up. Girls are going to be here soon." I glance up at the clock to confirm the time.

Opening the door felt like I was going to have a heart attack, and no, it wasn't because I straight sprinted when the doorbell went off. My heart was already beating out of my chest, so ready to see my girl.

Was she going to act shy in front of company, or was she going to be the dirty girl I'm fully obsessed with?

"Hey there, hot stuff." She grins while wrapping her arms around my neck.

"Hey Doll… Miss me yet?" Not letting her answer, I tilt her chin up to press my lips to hers, needing to feel them on me.

We get lost in the moment and by the time she releases my neck, I'm hard as fuck.

"Shiiittt, that was hot!" I hear Lottie say from behind us. I glance to see her cute face smiling at us in awe while G rests his arm around her shoulder, pressing a kiss to her temple.

He's giving me a smug-ass look, a look that basically screams 'you're so fucked, man.' Yeah, as if I didn't know that already.

Ashley picks up the bags that she had dropped at our feet and asks me to show her to the kitchen.

"You guys pick out the movie while we get the snacks ready!" she yells over her shoulder as I lead her in the right direction.

These girls certainly know how to pack for a hang-out sesh. Of course, they wouldn't settle for us providing everything for the night, and now I see why.

There's more variety of snacks here than there is at the local 7/11. I'm talking multiple kinds of chips with dip, candies ranging from Reece's pieces to sour worms, and let's not forget the plethora of trail mix. They came prepared.

"Damn girl, what did you buy, the whole damn convenience store?" I laugh as I continue to empty the bags onto the counter.

"Okay, so I kinda got a little stoned before we went into the store and once I was there, I couldn't decide. Everything looked so damn good. Then I got nervous that I didn't get things you guys wanted, so I went back and got more. Basically, I bought one of everything," she giggles.

I laugh at how cute she is. I can't help myself when I pull her body flush to mine and kiss her. She melts under my touch. I can feel her body relax along with my own. All the anxious energy I've been carrying all day floats away when she's near me.

"Hey! No fucking on the counters. I just cleaned that shit," I hear G yell from the den.

I smile against Ash's perfect lips.

"Cock block," I yell back.

Spinning her around, I swat at her ass. She gives me a devious smirk in response, and I have to adjust my semi before grabbing some of the food bowls.

"Come on, babe, let's get these into the living room."

She giggles as she grabs a tray, loads it with some snacks, and sashays away from me toward the couple on the couch. Luckily, I didn't hit anything on my way in, because I don't think I took my eyes off her ass the whole time.

We're about an hour and a half into our games, Heads Up being the current one, and I don't think I've laughed this much in a long time. We're all having a great night, laughing hysterically. Especially when G loses a round… punk ass is such a sore loser.

We've had some beers and smoked a joint or two, so we've made a decent dent into the snacks as well.

Honestly, I'm having such a good time hanging with Ashley, even G and Lottie, too. We talked about our plans for this week, including a pool party and G's birthday on the Fourth of July. We're all so fucking stoked for that. I think the girls already made a grocery list of the essentials.

I, for one, am by far the worst at this game. I blame Ash for that. She's too distracting. Her smile lights up the entire fucking room, and I can't help but stare at her face and memorize every expression that crosses it. I'm so fucked when it comes to this girl.

I call it quits when I fail to get any points two rounds in a row. I'm no quitter, but the idea of holding my girl close and watching a movie with her has me throwing the game cards down and pulling Ashley along with me.

She giggles as I lay her on the couch, grinding my hips into hers and placing a big kiss on her mouth. She parts her lips ever so slightly, granting me access to take it a bit further. Hearing Ashley moan softly when I move my hips against her again has me wishing we were alone.

Shit, if I don't stop now, my desire for her might win out over the whole 'no one is allowed to see what's mine' thing.

I lean back with a final peck to her lips as she stares at me with lust in her eyes. Situating us so we're on the reclining part of the large couch, I grab a blanket to drape over us.

"What did you guys pick out?" I question the duo on the opposite couch.

Lottie beams at me. "Only one of my personal favorites."

"*Superbad?*" Ashley questions knowingly.

"Abso-fricken-lutely!" she laughs.

Shaking my head, I open the app on my phone to turn down the lights. Did I forget to mention my spot has a killer setup?

I currently live in the pool house on my family's estate. My mom and dad surprised me with it on my eighteenth birthday. It was an unused building on our property, but they renovated it for me with no expenses spared. So, when I say this place is hooked up, I'm not lying.

They figured I'd want my own space when I'm home for college breaks and summer. I think they did this as an incentive for me to come home, since Trevor never did after he finished school.

I'm extremely grateful for their generosity. I love having my own space. It has several bedrooms as well, making it the perfect situation for G and me this summer.

Ashley snuggles up close as the movie starts. I love the feel of her body against mine.

"I'm glad you're here," I whisper softly to her.

She smiles softly at me. "I'm really glad I am too."

Leaning down, I place a soft kiss on her lips, hoping the connection expresses things I don't think I have the words for right now.

She rests her head on my chest as we watch the rest of the movie. Her hand gently strokes along my stomach and my arms and hands never fully leave her body, either.

I'm startled awake when I feel the cool air on my body replacing the warmth I've been wrapped in for the past few hours.

"Mmm, don't go," I murmur, trying to rub the sleep from my eyes.

"Shh, we have to, babe. I'm sorry." She places a kiss on my lips.

"Stay with me tonight. You don't have to go."

"I wish. Lottie's grandma Ethel has us scheduled for an early brunch tomorrow and if we're not bright-eyed and bushy-tailed for her, all hell breaks loose. Trust me, she's a real piece of work, and we try everything in our power to keep that woman sated."

"Sounds like a real peach."

"You don't know the half of it," she says, wrapping me into a huge hug. "But I'll see you at that pool party. Might need your help picking out what suit to wear. Maybe a little FaceTime fashion show is in order." She winks as she wiggles out of my grip.

"Don't you fucking tease me like that. There will be consequences." I grab my hardening cock to prove what she does to me.

Every. Fucking. Time.

"I'm looking forward to it, big guy." She winks and walks towards the door where G and Lottie are saying their goodbyes.

I throw my head back when I hear the door close behind them.

What am I going to do with this chick?

Chapter Nine

Trent

This pool party is just what I needed. The sun is shining brightly, the coolers are filled with an endless amount of beer, and the hottest chick here is smiling at me like she's about to devour me alive. *Bring it, baby!*

I can't stop myself from smiling back at her like the fool that I am. She looks so fucking stunning with her tanned skin and her black Baywatch-inspired one-piece. I love the fact that she doesn't have to wear a barely there two-piece to look sexy as fuck.

Honestly, every girl here stacked together doesn't even come close to how gorgeous Ashley truly is. Lottie is looking hot, too. Of course, I would never say that to G, for fear of losing my balls, but it's no less true. Our girls are fine.

Seeing the way the local chicks huddle together and talk about our girls makes me smile. Catty-ass bitches. Knowing neither of us has ever been exclusive to any chicks before has their claws out, I'm sure.

I made sure to stake my claim when we first arrived, giving my girl a long, drawn out kiss. We got a little carried away and her legs wound up wrapping around my body. I could feel the heat from between her legs, and if it wasn't for the catcalls, I might have made my girl's voyeuristic fantasies come true.

We've spent the better part of the time here playing games in the pool. Neither Ashley nor Lottie seem to be concerned with getting their hair wet, unlike the rest of the girls snarling from the sidelines.

G and Lottie are a force to be reckoned with in a Chicken Fight, even taking down some of our guy friend duos.

Ashley and I shined in the pool volleyball game. We made a perfect team, seemingly knowing what the other was about to do and exactly where to be to assist. It was awesome.

It's crazy to think this girl was practically a stranger to me before the summer started, and now I can't imagine what life is going to be like after this week.

It's not something I want to think about, but the thoughts are there, nonetheless. Constantly begging me to bring it up to Ashley, but I don't want to risk this week going sour. I'm enjoying it too much.

Smiling back from our chairs, G and I watch as Ashley and Lottie play an intense game of beer pong.

Not paying attention to anything but my girl, I feel a hand glide over my shoulder. Looking up, I see Felicity with her painted-on red lips and face full of makeup. Does she know we're at a pool party? Ugh, knowing I used to fuck this chick has my skin crawling.

"Hey there, hot stuff, haven't seen you all day," she purrs into my ear.

That's a blatant lie. I know damn well she was close by when Ashley and I had our make-out session earlier. She was part of the reason I did it. Even though I haven't touched this chick in a few months, I didn't want her to think there was any chance of us happening today, or in the future, for that matter.

Removing her hand from my shoulder, I respond, "Oh, hey. Didn't realize you were here today."

"Of course, we're here! We wouldn't want to miss one of Nathan's epic pool parties."

Nathan is a cool guy. We graduated together and hang out occasionally. We've been hanging out more than usual this summer because he's been working with G at The Shack. He's good people.

"No, of course you wouldn't." I turn back around from this fake conversation to see our girls doing a celebratory dance. G is already headed over towards them with new beers for their next game.

"Where have you been? Haven't seen you around lately?" Felicity asks the back of my head.

Why is she still here?

"Been around. My girl's in town, so I've been spending all my time on her."

Yeah, I know what I said, and I mean it too. I don't want to give Felicity any hope of us hooking up.

"Oh, I didn't realize you have a girl. Since when is big man Trent Manning a one-woman type of guy?" she says as she slides her hand down my biceps.

"Since I found someone worthy enough to make me." I practically growl as I remove her hand for the second time.

"She's pretty. I wouldn't mind joining you," she croons.

"Yeah, that's not going to fucking happen. I won't be sharing her anytime soon."

"Mmm, well, then let me know when she's not around. I could use a good dick session and only you can give me what I need," she adds, trailing her fingertips up my neck.

"I think you heard him the first time he turned you down." I hear my girl say from the other side of me. Smiling to myself, loving the jealousy and take no shit tone in her voice. "Now, move," Ashley says, stepping closer so Felicity has no choice but to move out of her way.

"Ugh, whatever." A stunned Felicity retreats to her swarm of girls, throwing glaring looks over her shoulder at the two of us.

"Thanks for rescuing me." I pull Ashley's warm body onto my lap. Gripping her chin and kissing her so deeply, she moans.

"No problem, big guy. I just needed to make sure she knew what's up. I overheard her practically throwing herself at you and thought she needed a little more proof you weren't interested."

"You know… if I didn't know any better, I would think you were a little jealous. Is that it, Doll? Did seeing her hands on me get the best of you?"

Ashley

Jealous? Fucking jealous doesn't even come close to how I felt. I was ready to rip that girl's extensions right out of her damn hair if her hand lingered any more on my man.

Geez, what the hell has he done to me? I'm not usually like this. I'm the carefree, free-love type of girl, not the protective lioness with sharpened claws.

Thinking quickly, I grab his hand and motion with my head for him to follow my lead. I saw a pool house earlier on the other side of the yard that will suit my needs just fine.

It just so happens that to get to said pool house, we need to pass Malibu Barbie and all her cronies.

I feel them all staring.

It seems quite obvious what my intentions are. They definitely think I'm going to bang T in the outdoor shower. Fine with me. Let them think whatever they'd like… It's probably true, anyway.

Peering back at him and his goofy-ass smile has me laughing. He knows damn well I'm jealous, and he's loving every moment of it. *Jerk!*

We make it to the pool house, and I look for my intended destination. When I see it, I pull his hand eagerly. Aah, the outdoor shower.

"Wipe that stupid grin off of your face," I growl at him, closing and locking the shower door behind us.

It's way more private inside than I thought it would be. The wooden enclosure has some openings, but not enough for people to see inside. Did I mention it's also fully stocked in here, with a wooden bench, a basket full of towels, and a shelf filled with all the shower essentials?

"How could I not be smiling right now? I have the finest girl here, marking her territory by pulling me away to a secluded spot." I smile at his assessment.

Trent tucks a piece of hair behind my ear, then cups my chin so our eyes meet.

"It's okay, baby. I would have done the same thing if the situation was flipped." He places a gentle kiss on my cheek. My stomach does that weird twisty thing at his words.

"Now, what was going through that pretty mind of yours when you dragged me away from the party?" He places a kiss on my neck while reaching behind us, turning on the water.

Tilting my head to give him better access to my neck, I whimper when he licks along the side of my throat.

"Oh, you'll find out soon enough."

Placing my hands on the string of his swim trunks, I start to untie them. I need to feel him. Need him to know that he drives me crazy with want.

Freeing the tie, I drop down to my knees, taking his shorts along with me. I'm greeted by his long shaft.

Licking my lips, I stare up at him, locking eyes with his. *Fuck, he's hot.*

"Someone is excited to see me," I joke as I wrap my fingers around him and give him a slow stroke.

"Mmm, I'm always excited to see you. But what are you going to do about it?" he questions as he steps out of his shorts, leaving him gloriously naked for me to ogle.

The sight of his naked form with water cascading around him has me throbbing.

Trent reaches behind me and grabs something. Next thing I know, he is throwing a towel down for me to kneel on.

After repositioning myself onto the folded towel, I grip him once more.

"Do you know how much I love this cock of yours?" I say as I lick the tip.

"Fuuckk. Show me, Doll… Show me how much you love it." He grips the back of my ponytail, not hard enough to hurt, but just enough to prove how much he's into this.

I wrap my lips around the tip and work my mouth down his shaft, loving the way his body shudders as I do.

I work his cock with my fist and mouth, the perfect combination, twisting and slurping. Driving him fucking crazy.

His grip on my hair has tightened a bit, but he's letting me have all the control right now, which is sexy as hell.

With my other hand, I gently palm his balls and massage them. His legs are twitching, and I know he won't last much longer. Trent lets out a stream of incoherent words, making me smile around his dick.

"Shit, oh shit! I'm going to come down that gorgeous little throat of yours," he manages to say between grunts.

I feel his hand push just as his dick pulses with his release down my throat, just like he said. I make sure to lick him clean, teasing his sensitive tip.

He grips my cheeks and smirks. "Fuck, that was… One hell of a skill set."

Standing up, I blush at his praise, remembering that particular text conversation. He wraps his arms around me, kissing my lips, and drags us beneath the shower stream.

Trent's hands go to my shoulder at the same time his lips do, and before you know it, he has both of my bathing suit straps down. His delicious mouth places open kisses on the sensitive skin of my collarbone.

I'm aching with need, his lips setting my body on fire.

He stops abruptly, and I moan in frustration when I hear a female voice from the other side of the door.

"Are you almost done in there? Some of us would like to use the shower."

We both silently laugh at the attitude coming from the door.

"Be out in a minute," Trent yells.

Disappointment fills me, knowing I'm going to have an aching center for the rest of the day.

Trent leans down to whisper in my ear, "Don't you worry, baby, I won't let you ache for too long."

I groan in frustration.

"I'm counting on it." I wink as I fix my hair, knowing it probably resembles a rat's nest.

He wraps a dry towel around me and then dresses himself. Grabbing my hand, he opens the shower door. "Come on, let's go. I want to take you somewhere special."

When we look up, we are greeted by a very pissed-off Felicity, who's standing there with her hip cocked and hands crossed over her set of large tits. I just smirk at her and walk right back to the party, hand in hand with my man.

I smile inwardly when I hear her huff out in frustration. Good… lesson learned, bitch.

He.

Is.

Mine.

But how am I supposed to keep him?

After dropping Lottie and G back at their place, Trent made sure to stay true to his promise. Let me tell you, the back seat of a Jeep is roomier than one might assume.

Now that I can no longer feel my toes, it's time to eat.

I'm craving some fried seafood and a milkshake, so we head to one of Trent's favorite takeout spots, which happens to be the same place I discovered my love of shrimp burgers three summers ago.

It's a cute mom-and-pop type of place and considering the line is wrapped around the building, it's safe to say Big Oak is a local favorite.

With our bags full of fries and fresh-caught shrimp on a bun, we drive to Trent's special spot. Thankfully, it's not long before he's pulling off onto a short dirt road.

Hopping out, we grab a blanket from the back and head over to the lookout.

The sun is setting in the distance and the picturesque views take my breath away.

From here I can see the bustling boardwalk along with the beautiful sand and ocean. The orange hue of the sky as the sun sets makes it that much more impressive.

"Wow, it's gorgeous up here."

Trent comes to stand next to me, stretching out his arms. "Yeah, it's one of my favorite spots to come and just chill. I'm glad you like it."

"Like it? I love it... I feel like I'm in my own world here. It's amazing. Thank you for bringing me here, I guess it pays to be banging a local." I wink at him with a stupid grin on my face. Wrapping my arms around his waist, I nestle my head into his chest.

After a few moments of silence, he speaks up, "Come on, let's eat. Our food is getting cold and I don't want to hear your stomach growling anymore. She sounds hangry."

I swat at his arm. "She's not hangry!" I pat my belly. "We just know good food when we smell it!"

Nothing has ever felt as right as I do right now, sitting on the blanket snuggled up next to Trent with our full bellies from the delicious food. The sun setting ahead of us, turning the sky into a magnificent array of colors.

I look over at Trent, who's already staring in my direction. His eyes filled with questions I know I probably don't want to answer, but I ask anyway.

"What are you thinking?" I ask as I stare at his gorgeous face.

"I'm wondering how I got so lucky running into you at Masqued." He smirks at me. "Think about it... Of all the places in New York my brother could have taken me to, he took me there."

"Yeah, the universe sure is funny that way, isn't it?" I retort. The universe and I are currently at an awkward standstill in my mind.

"Do you believe in fate?" he asks.

"You know... I never really thought about it up until recently," I answer truthfully.

"Put it this way, I was never supposed to work at Masqued. I entered a competition for costume design through a program at my high school. Sloan, the owner of Masqued, saw some of my designs at the show and asked me if I'd be interested in drawing up a couple of options for the new club she was opening."

"Really? Wow, they must have been something special if she asked you privately to draw up something for her?" He beams at me with pride.

"Yeah, I guess so." I smile back.

"Okay, so explain this to me then. If you were just designing outfits for Masqued, how did you start working there?"

"Sloan asked me to come in to see Masqued so I could get a feel for the club to help with my design inspirations. It wasn't open yet, but the staff was there training, and the interior was basically completed. My first thought when I walked through the door was damn, I need to work here. The vibe was exactly what I needed at that time. I wanted an escape from my reality, and Masqued gave me that. So, after I completed my costume design ideas for Sloan, I asked for a job. Of course, being that I was only eighteen then, I had my restrictions, but we made it work."

"Wait… so did she use your designs for the uniform?" Trent asks. I love that he pays attention to every detail.

"Yes, she did."

"Fuck me, I dreamt about you in that outfit for weeks." He groans.

"Oh really? I have plenty more mockups where that came from, I'll have to give you a show." I wink at him.

"Okay, so if you love designing so much, why don't you try going to school or taking up an internship?" he questions.

"Again, it's something I've been thinking about more lately. Even though I love Masqued and the escape it provided me, I regret not applying to fashion school. Working there just doesn't feel the same anymore." He doesn't have to know it's because I no longer feel anonymous there. Gio's men are closing in. I can feel it.

"I get that. So, what are you thinking then?"

"Honestly, there's a program at a college in Manhattan that I was considering applying to. They have a great fashion design program. I just need to get my portfolio together." I just hope it's something I can pursue even with my impending nuptials.

"I'm proud of you babe. If your designs are anything like the costume at Masqued, they'd be fools not to accept you," he says, settling the anxious bubble forming in my gut.

I lean over to place a kiss on his lips. He always knows exactly the right words to say to make me feel better.

Damn, I'm falling for this man. I am so screwed.

Needing to change the subject immediately, I ask, "So what about you? Have you always wanted to be a doctor?"

Through our countless texting, this is something he has mentioned quite a few times, making sure I know he will be attending NYU in the fall.

"Yeah, I've dreamt of it ever since I was a kid. My dad is a surgeon, and my brother has a private practice in Manhattan. Well, at least I think he does."

I give him a puzzled look.

"Let's just say I think he's taken on a specific clientele and we'll leave it at that."

I don't question any further because he doesn't push me for explanations either, and I want to show him the same respect.

"That's awesome. I'm proud of you for pursuing your dreams. Do you know what field you want to go into?"

"I'm not sure just yet, but I'm leaning more towards surgery."

We fall into silence after that, watching the remaining glow of the sun disappear beyond the horizon.

Trent takes our entwined hands and lifts the back of mine to his lips, kissing so gently it almost brings tears to my eyes. His gaze locks with mine.

"You know, I never gave fate a second thought either, not until seeing you here at my house five months after the club. Before that, I thought of you every night… I was so mad when little details started to fade, but the feeling, the immediate connection, never went away." I can't take my eyes off him when he's being so candid like this.

"Then that night of the party, I felt it again while staring at a little blonde vixen dancing around my living room. I thought maybe she would be the one to finally take my mind off Maggie and then it was you. How can we not believe in fate at this point?"

My phone buzzes with a text. Not wanting to disrupt our moment, I ignore it. The surrounding air is thick with lust and maybe even something I'm not yet ready to discuss…

He takes the back of my neck into his palm and kisses me deeply. I immediately wrap my arms around his shoulders to get closer. Our tongues tangle together in a feverishly erotic way, making me throb with need once again.

I don't think I could ever get tired of the way he makes me feel, mind, body, and soul.

His phone starts to ring, forcing us to break apart. He growls in frustration and excuses himself while he answers it.

"Yo!" he barks into the phone.

"Really man…"

"All right, chill the fuck out. Hold on, let me ask."

He turns to me, muting the phone.

"It's G, Lottie's buzzed and wants to go to the boardwalk's amusement park and since it's one of your last nights here, she wants to know if we would like to meet them there?"

I contemplate for a moment. I would like to spend some more alone time with Trent, but a double date at the boardwalk does sound like a lot of fun.

"Don't worry, you're sleeping over at my spot tonight, so we will still have our time," he adds, knowing I'm conflicted. *How does he always know?*

I smile up at him. "All of that sounds perfect!"

"You sure? No pressure," he says, quirking an eyebrow.

I nod.

He unmutes G. "Yeah, we'll meet you. What time?"

"Oh, you're there already… Okay, we'll see you soon." He ends the call.

He grabs my hand once more, kissing it, sending a tingle to my toes.

"Sorry to cut this short, but they're already there. They went to eat at The Shack. Are you okay with packing it up now? I mean, I could call him back and tell him to fuck off."

"Haha! No, we can head there now, but only if you promise to make it up to me later." I grin devilishly at him.

"Always, baby girl, always," he answers with a smug-as-fuck look on his face.

Cocky bastard.

But I'm not going to lie, I look forward to it.

Chapter Ten

Ashley

"WAHOOOOO!" Lottie yells, looking over at me, both our hair blowing in the wind and arms up in the air. We're sitting up on top of the backseat of Trent's jeep as he drives us onto the beach.

Grabbing a hold of her hand in the air, I say, "Thank you… I needed this vacation. It feels fucking amazing to just let loose, doesn't it?"

This has been one of the best weeks of my life.

Smiling back at me, she yells, "YESSS! It's perfect." She leans forward and rubs the top of Greyson's head. "And so is my birthday boy… Happy birthday, baby!"

He smiles back at her, shaking his head at our silly antics. I love seeing how happy my bestie is. I've never seen her this way… so herself and in love. I just hope no one gets hurt when it's time to go back to reality at the end of the summer.

Even through the dark lenses of Trent's sunglasses, I can feel his eyes on me in the rearview mirror.

"Eyes on the road T… or should I say, the beach. You gotta keep your precious cargo safe," I scold jokingly from my seat.

He kisses the air with his lips while looking in the mirror. "Always baby."

The guys picked an awesome place on the beach for our camping site. It's away from the crowd, a "local spot," as they called it.

It was sexy as hell watching them get all manly as they put up our tents for the night.

Thanks to Trent's mom, our cooler is stacked to the brim with a bunch of yummy food. The guys plan to start a bonfire at dusk so we can roast hotdogs and enjoy our mini feast.

It's going to be a good day.

There is absolutely nothing like laying on the beach with your toes in the sand, sipping a cold one, with some good tunes playing. I haven't been this much at peace inside my head in a long time. Lottie is passed out beside me, probably worn out from her long night in the sheets.

Luckily, her evil grandmother went out of town for the weekend, so we didn't have to answer to her yesterday or today, which meant we slept over at the guys' place. I cooked a big pot of sauce and meatballs for us, and Lottie baked us some cookies. We took advantage of the large pool and went for a late-night swim. Then we all went our separate ways, and let's just say we both had a ten out of ten recommend kinda night.

Needless to say, we're all pretty worn out today from our sleepover—or lack thereof.

Trent and Greyson don't seem tired at all, though.

T insisted on bringing out their old skim boards from when they were younger in honor of Greyson's birthday, and they have been at it for an hour already. You could tell the minute they first tried them out and realized they weren't twelve-year-old boys anymore... it's not quite as easy when you are over six feet of pure muscle. Lottie and I had some good laughs out of it, though.

I normally love a crowd because it helps keep me out of my head, but I have to say today I am truly enjoying the fact that Greyson wanted a low-key birthday. I don't want to share my people with anyone else.

My people... it feels good to be able to say that.

Trent has quickly become someone I can't ever see *not* being in my life, but I know it won't be in the capacity that I want it to be.

He is so full of goodness, something I feel there's not enough of in my life.

Don't get me wrong the other day shined some light on his old fuck boy ways, but I have never felt misled or questioned his desire for me. He's always optimistic and kind, he even asks genuine questions to get to know me.

He is everything that every woman deserves and everything I'll never have. Today, I'm pretending though... *he is mine*!

At least for another twenty-four hours. Does this really end after tomorrow? I don't see any other way this can go.

No matter how much I try to keep my feelings in check, it's impossible when it comes to him. I was so stupid thinking this week would fix our need for each other. When, in reality, all it has done is show me exactly what I'll never have but desperately want and need.

I don't want to hurt him, and I certainly don't want to put him in danger. But how can I let him go, knowing damn well he won't give up easily unless I ask him to?

Slick. Wet. Hard.

Mmm, the hot-body walking my way strips my racing thoughts away.

Damn, that boy is fine.

"Don't you look like the poster boy for Boys Down East right now?" I say, pretending to fan myself.

He smirks, leaning in to kiss me. "And you look a little hot... want another *Truly*, or do you need to go to the bathhouse for a cold shower?" I love his smart-ass comebacks, but I'll never tell him that.

"Shut up! It's the sun making me sweat. Want to go for a swim with me?" I jump and start to run towards the water, yelling behind me, "Last one to the water has to do ten burpees on the beach."

I hear him coming after me but thankfully the water isn't far away and I win... ya girl isn't doing no damn burpees on the beach.

But watching my man's muscles and body move up and down while he does them... I'll take that.

Right as I get past the wave break, he catches up to me and dunks me under, quickly pulling me back up and saying, "That's for cheating! And this is for getting a head start." He picks me up and twirls me around, tossing me back into the water.

"You know damn well I'd be watching your ass bounce as you ran ahead of me. I call that an unfair advantage," he says as he pulls me into him and l open without hesitation. His kisses send shivers all over my body.

I consider begging him to take me right here in the ocean, but I know Lottie has plans for G later, so we will get our alone time tonight, and besides, the buildup between us is always fun.

I'm startled awake when a large hand grabs my breast and something hard grinds into my ass. The delicious smell of Trent surrounds me, and I smile.

I had crawled into the tent after the sun finally wore me out to take a much-needed afternoon catnap. A few moments later, I felt his big body come in and snuggle up behind me. The breeze on the beach was flowing in perfectly through the tent windows and I was out within minutes.

I grind back into Trent, letting him know I'm awake and down for whatever he's offering. He doesn't waste any time and slides his hands under the cover-up I'm wearing and down to my bikini bottoms. Just as his finger rubs through my wet folds and he groans, Lottie pokes her head in the tent with an oh shit look on her face. "Uh shit, sorry! I can't exactly knock, and I didn't hear anything, so I thought it was safe to wake you guys. It's time to start the fire, Trent."

T and I both bust out laughing at Lottie's discomfort and tell her we'll be out in a second.

I turn in his arms and give him a long kiss laced with promises for later. "Let's go help them. We will get our fun tonight."

He growls at me but agrees, probably only because he knows it's Greyson's birthday.

Trent stands up, adjusting himself to hide his hard-on in his swim trunks.

"If you're that wet from a little grinding, I can't wait to see you dripping down your leg by tonight, Doll." My dirty boy winks.

An hour later, the fire is roaring, and we've just finished eating our hotdogs, along with some delicious potato salad and coleslaw that Mrs. Manning made for us.

Lottie is busy setting up stuff for s'mores because what's a bonfire without s'mores, right?

She puts one marshmallow on the stick and looks at G. "The birthday boy gets the first one. Do you like yours crispy or just warm?" My best friend is so smitten.

"Burn'er Babygirl!" He says with a wink to his girl. As Lottie roasts the big white puff, a debate starts between all of us about what foods are better burnt.

Tig gets the marshmallow, chocolate, and graham cracker all prepared and then looks to Trent and me, who on cue, start to sing "Happy Birthday" to Greyson.

He is a broody guy who doesn't say much unless it's to Lottie, but you can tell how much he appreciates the little things like this. He pulls her to him and onto his lap as she finishes singing "Happy birthday" to him, whispering lovingly in his ear.

After we are all chocolate wasted, Tig and G head out to get to their spot before the fireworks start.

Trent looks at me once they're out of sight. "Man, I love my cousin, but I am so glad to finally have you to myself. It's dark, no one is anywhere near us… the possibilities are endless."

Smacking his arm as I laugh, I say, "That wasn't creepy or anything."

He stands with a devilish grin in place. "Ya know? I have the perfect place for us to watch the fireworks, too."

Having no idea what he has up his sleeve, but before I can respond, he leans down and picks me up, throwing me over his shoulder and running down towards the ocean.

"Nope. No Sir! Trent, I mean it! I'll gut you!" I yell as I pound on his back.

He smacks my ass. "Come on, it's just your cover-up. Who cares if our clothes get wet?"

"I don't care about the clothes, you idiot. It's the sharks. I've always heard they come near the shore at night!" He laughs and keeps moving forward. My measly hits aren't affecting him one bit.

"Come on Doll, you know I won't let anything happen to you. I'd even wrestle Jaws for you," he says as I hear his feet hit the water.

I can't help but laugh at his comment because he probably would. It hits me how he is just as fearless as a made man, which is actually kind of terrifying. I have little time to think about that before I'm taken under with him.

Just like before, he pulls me up quickly and kisses me. I can't help but feed off his carefree and fun vibe.

Putting me on my feet in the ocean, he leans back, most likely checking to see that I'm not ready to kick him in his nuts. It gives me the chance to see him in the moonlight with his wet, white t-shirt clinging perfectly to his muscular chest and shoulders. He is like a sexy wet dream.

"Ashley, do you realize how beautiful you are? Seeing you like this," he pauses, shaking his head. "You're perfect, baby."

If I wasn't already about to climb him like a tree, the loud boom just down the beach has me jumping into his arms and wrapping my legs around him. Realizing it's the fireworks, he turns our bodies so we can watch them as we hold one another.

I don't think I have ever experienced fireworks like this. I feel like we're in our own little world right now.

I am pretty sure there has never been a more perfect Fourth of July and probably never will be.

Looking up at Trent, I get caught up in the moment and the feelings this man brings out in me. I grab his face and pull him down to me until his lips meet mine. This kiss is unlike anything I have ever experienced in my life. It's like we are saying all the things we can't out loud.

From the moment we locked eyes in that club, this crazy chemistry has been there and it's intoxicating.

One more day isn't long enough, it never will be.

Trent

We're both out of our minds and so worked up for each other at this moment. Needing to take a breath, I pull away before I embarrass myself.

But Ash is not wasting any time. She takes my hand and leads me towards the shoreline.

Before I know it, she's pushed me onto the wet sand and is on top of me, pulling at the laces of my swim trunks. I lift my ass off the ground to help her get my trunks down.

She groans out when she sees my hard dick jut into the air.

"Shit Trent, you don't know how bad I need you right now," she says as she pulls her bikini bottom to the side and grabs my dick with her other hand, sliding the tip through her sex.

Seeing her like this, crazed and unable to wait any longer, is probably the sexiest thing I have ever seen.

"Oh, but I do, because I need and want you even more." Right when she lines herself up with my dick, I push my hips up into her.

"Fuckkkk, your pussy feels so damn good." She grinds herself onto me, rocking her hips. "That's it… ride my cock."

And she does.

She surprises me by taking what seemed like a quick fuck and turning it into something slow and connected, never taking her eyes off mine.

We both moan and groan. Her pace quickens but if I didn't know any better, I would think she was making love to me.

I let her stay in control, taking in every second of my girl. Only moving my eyes down from hers to watch her take my cock inside her sweet pussy.

"Baby, you are killing me. How does this feel so good?" I growl my thoughts out loud.

Ash leans closer to me, looking into my eyes and grinding her pussy down onto me while she rotates her hips just how she needs it. I can see the fire in her eyes. She is close, so close.

"Trent baby, I'm going to come, fuuuck." It's the first time she has taken her eyes away from mine. They roll back in her head, and she lets go.

Fucking. Ecstasy.

"That's right, come all over my cock… Fuck, I can feel you milking me."

Not being able to help it, I flip her over so her back is on the wet sand. I lift her coverup just enough to pull her swollen breast from her top so I can suck on it as I ride out my high.

When my mouth grabs onto her nipple, her back lifts off the sand. "Yes Trent, yes!"

Uncontrollably fucking her as my knees dig into the sand, I feel her start to squeeze me again and I know we are both about to explode.

"I'm about to fill you up baby, come with me… now!"

That does it for both of us.

Moaning, writhing, scratching as we both come undone.

Getting our breathing under control, I brace my weight on my forearms, leaning down to give her a gentle kiss.

"Damn, what was that?" I say, rolling off her. Both of us lay on our backs in the wet sand, not giving a fuck.

"That… that was the perfect combination of making love and fucking," she says, looking up at the sky.

Surprised she admitted that, I go to speak and confess what I really want to, but her pleading eyes stop me. So instead, I take her face with my hands and say, "I want you." Kissing her gently, I add, "Always."

She smiles sadly at me and whispers, "Me too baby… me too."

We both release a big sigh, letting all of our unspoken words drift off into the night sky.

Trying to make light of the situation, she takes one out of my playbook.

Ash looks at me with a cocky grin. "You know I had sex on the beach last year for the first time... but it didn't involve so much sand."

Even though I'm pretty sure she's just messing with me, I turn over quickly, getting into her face as I growl, "What did you just say to me?"

She smiles widely, pushing at my chest "I meant the drink dummy... The drink was actually nowhere near as good as the real thing sans the sand."

"Oh, you are in trouble for that one, Doll," I say as I tickle her to tears.

Coming out of the bathhouse, I find Ash already finished and sitting on top of my Jeep, deep in thought. My stomach fills with dread as I climb up to sit beside her and see the look on her face.

Grabbing her hand to soothe her, she speaks before I have the chance to. "You were supposed to be fun. You weren't supposed to be so much more."

Her eyes fill with tears, and I pull her to me. "Baby, tell me what you need. I'll do anything for you. I'll fight any battle if it means I get to keep you in my life. Just tell me what we're fighting against."

Her face is full of agony. "Trent, I'm promised to someone else."

I feel like someone just sucker-punched me with her revelation. Having a hard time controlling myself, I say, "What the fuck do you mean? Promised to someone else... this is the twenty-first century Ashley."

She grabs my arm as I go to stand, needing some space. "Please, let me talk."

Turning to listen to her, she goes on. "I'm promised to a man I have never met. We will be wed when I turn twenty-one. Our fathers are… business associates, and they have made this deal without our permission. I have no say in the matter." She pauses to gather her thoughts.

"Going against this arrangement could jeopardize so many things in my life. It puts the people I love in danger and that's not something I'm willing to do. The risk is too great."

Seeing my brain work and knowing I'm trying to put the pieces together, she places her finger on my lips. "T please don't ask me things I cannot tell you. Just know that my father loves me, but he is associated with some dangerous people. Unfortunately for me, I have to reap what has been sown by others."

What the fuck is her family caught up in? I thought this kind of shit was only in the movies.

"Is Lottie caught up in this shit, too?" I ask.

"God no! Although her family is fucked up, her situation is very different from my own."

I pace back and forth, trying to compose myself. "Ash, this is fucked. There has to be something we can do."

"No Trent, please don't make me regret telling you this. Just give me the rest of tonight to enjoy our time together. A time I'll hold on to during the dark days. You help me forget the responsibilities of my future and make me feel like the fun, free-spirited teenager I want to be, and for that, I am forever grateful. Please give me one more night of that."

The pleading look in her eyes pulls at my heartstrings.

My emotions are all over the place, but I know one thing for sure; I don't want to take a second of my time with her for granted.

Sitting back down beside her on the hood of my Jeep, I pull her into me. Wrapping my arms around her body.

"Okay baby, what do you want to do?"

"Just hold me, make love to me, kiss me, talk to me… everything. I don't need any sleep. I just want to spend every moment until my plane leaves tomorrow caught up in you."

I kiss her temple and hold on to her tightly.

"Trent… You make me feel so much. It scares the hell out of me to admit that, but you deserve to know that no matter what, I will always remember you and these precious moments."

She starts to get choked up, but continues, "I want you to be so successful and live out every single one of your dreams. Even though I don't even want to think about this, I do want you to know that someday you are going to make a lucky girl so fucking happy. Please don't ever settle for anything less than someone who treats you like the King you are."

"Baby Doll, it would always be settling if it wasn't you," I say as I grip her chin, leaning in to kiss her.

"You're perfect, Trent. If anything in my life ever changes and you still feel that way, I promise I will find my way to you."

"I'll take that promise," I say, taking her hand to my chest. "For now, I will respect what you're asking of me, but know I am here at the drop of a dime. Fate brought us together twice now. I'll hold on to the fact that it will bring us back to one another again someday."

I peck her on the lips. "You know what they say… Third times a charm," I say, trying to ease some of the worry on her pretty face, but internally knowing I will find a way to have her.

Ashley licks her lips, smiling back at me, whispering softly, "I miss you already."

Epilogue

Ashley

I have done a lot of soul-searching this past month.

I still don't have a solid solution to my inevitable marriage to a man I don't want or even know. But my brother swears there is something in the works. I just hope that comes to fruition sooner than later.

Regardless, I do have a plan for my happiness in the right here and now… That is if he accepts my offer.

I have never wanted something or someone as badly as I want Trent. The last thirty-three days without him in my life have been way too dark. I need his light soul, his perfect body, and his fire-starting touch… I need him, anyway I can get him.

So that's why I've come up with an idea… an arrangement of sorts.

Today is Friday, the one day of the week I never feel watchful eyes on me. That's because it is the designated day that all made men in the area meet up at Gio's club, Sinners, and discuss "family" business.

Fridays are my day… and hopefully soon, *our* day to be free.

Stepping out of my Uber, I grab my papers and check my phone to confirm the location Lottie sent me.

Thank God for her having an in with Greyson. Thanks to them, I know exactly where Trent's freshmen orientation is taking place today.

Unfortunately, it seems like something is going on with Lottie. Knowing her, she probably isn't telling me because she knows how excited I am about today.

She seemed so down on the phone the other day and then when I asked about G, it sounded like she got choked up. I hung up and tried to FaceTime her immediately, knowing she can't lie to my face, but she wouldn't answer.

Lottie responded via text, telling me she was fine, but that the reality of the summer being over was hitting her hard. Thankfully, she'll be back in New York soon. I miss her like crazy.

Approaching the courtyard in front of the student union where I was told they would be meeting today for orientation, I spot an enormous crowd of anxious freshmen.

They all seem very nervous, well, all except one.

There's one tall, sexy guy with piercing green eyes who appears not only cool, calm, and collected among the rest, but like he's been waiting for this day his whole life.

Seeing plenty of attractive girls near him has me rethinking this entire plan. Knowing damn well he will have the pick of the litter here. *Ugh, don't go there, Ash. You want him to be happy. There is no reason both of you need to be unhappy your whole lives.*

"Holy Fuck," comes from the deep voice I have grown to love, snapping me out of my thoughts as he walks away from the crowd and heads toward me.

He looks at me like I'm not real, like I'm some sort of mirage.

"Baby, I felt you, but I honestly thought my mind was playing tricks on me," he says as his hand goes to the back of my head and pulls me into a big bear hug. He whispers in my ear, "I want to kiss you so badly."

Pulling back enough to go on my tippy toes, I show him just how badly I want that too. He immediately opens for me and our tongues touch, reigniting the fire that always burns so strongly between us.

Breaking for air because I know we don't have much time, all I can do is stare at him in awe.

"Did you miss me, Baby?" He smirks as he grabs onto my hips possessively.

"EVERY single part of me has missed you tremendously this last month, but before we get you a reputation on campus, we need to stop." I swat at his arm playfully.

He laughs discreetly, grinding his hard-on into my front. "Me too Doll, me too. I still can't believe you're here. I want to say fuck orientation and be with you the rest of the day."

A sense of relief washes over me. I'm feeling even more hopeful about my proposition with how he's responding to my surprise visit.

I was super anxious since I'm the one who asked for us to stop all communication so that I could let him move on while I worked out my own shit.

Now that I have, I can't help but hope it's not too late.

"No sir, you worked too hard to be here and I will never stand in the way of your dreams coming true. Especially not when you inspired me to follow my own."

I grin at him as I open up the paper I've been holding to show him its contents. A huge smile spreads across his face.

"NO FUCKING WAY!" he says, picking me up and twirling me around before setting me back down on my feet.

"You did it! You got into fashion school. I knew you could do it, no question! I'm so damn proud of you for going after it, baby. You are going to do big things."

Man, it feels so good to have him in my corner and know he truly believes in me. *He really is my person.*

"Thank you for believing in me. Seeing how passionate you are about your goals really pushed me to go after my own."

Before he can respond, someone calls out over the megaphone, telling the freshmen they need to be in their assigned areas within the next few minutes.

I take advantage of the little time we have, handing him the second piece of paper I have in my hand, except this one is in an envelope.

"Read this when you have the time, think on it, and well… the rest is up to you." I can tell the envelope has thrown him off, so I lean up again to give him a peck on the lips.

"Go have a good orientation day, T. It was so good to see your handsome face. I have missed you so much."

Trent

The saying "I hate to see her go but I love to watch her leave" has never resonated with me quite like it does right now. *Damn, my girl has the perfect ass.*

I felt her the minute she walked up today, but I told myself that it was just my hope of being in New York and closer to her playing tricks on me.

I swear I think she got even more beautiful since the last time I saw her.

Just the sight of her brings out feelings that scare the shit out of me. And this envelope... I'm jittery just thinking about what's inside it.

I know I can't wait till lunch, so I make up an excuse to go to the bathroom and tell the upperclassmen in charge of my group that I will meet them at the next spot on our itinerary.

I can't open the envelope fast enough.

> Trent,
>
> It was never a question of missing you. In fact, I missed you when you were a complete stranger to me after our first night together at Masqued. Now that nagging feeling of missing you has turned into a constant need and want for you.
>
> That brings me to why I'm writing this letter. I'm going to ask something of you. I'm going to be selfish a little while longer. Friday nights, starting tonight, will you meet me at the W a few blocks from your school, and spend the night with

me? It's the one night a week I don't have to answer to anyone.

Even though I want to with every fiber of my being, I can't give you anything more at this time and you must agree not to ask that of me. If by any chance my situation changes, you will be the first to know, but for now, this is all I can offer. So, I want you to really think about this and if you would rather move forward with your life, I will completely understand. I just want you to be happy, and I truly mean that.

If you choose to meet me. Then my Friday nights are all yours to do with as you please :)

Room 865
9 pm
I want you... Always,
Ash xox

At 8:59 pm I knock on the door of room 865 because there is no way I am letting my girl think for even a second that I'm not coming.

With the knowledge of what awaits me on the other side of this door, my dick is already hard and ready.

Ashley opens the door, a mix of emotions on her face. Looking into her eyes, my favorite shade of blue, I see the relief and excitement that shines in them at me being here.

My cock jerks in my pants at the sight of her because it feels like a lifetime ago since I've seen her like this.

She pulls me into the room wearing her black lace mask and uniform, just like the first night I met her at Masqued.

All kinds of overwhelming emotions wash over me at the knowledge that I still get to be with Ashley, even if it's in secret.

Moving my stare down to her lips, I can't wait any longer. Putting my mouth to hers, I slowly take in her taste.

This kiss isn't about the dirty things I know we will do to each other tonight. It's about me showing her exactly how much I've missed her and how thankful I am that she is giving me this.

Knowing we both need air, I reluctantly break away, but she leans up on her tippy toes and plants one more soft peck on my lips as she says, "I want you… Always."

"Same baby, same."

"So that's a yes for Fridays, Mr. Manning?" she says in a sultry-as-fuck tone as she pushes me down on the bed.

Oh yeah, I'm really into this.

"Baby Doll, you should know with you the answers always yes."

Walking over to her phone, she completes the scene by turning on a sensual beat as she starts to dance her way back over to me. Moving her hips as only she can, I can't wait to feel them roll like that as she rides my dick tonight.

Dropping onto my lap with her back to me. I run my finger down her spine, over those words that I love.

"What does this mean?" I don't want to ruin the moment, but I've thought about it so often over the past month, and I have to ask.

"I got it not long after my parents told me about my arrangement. I knew that someday something good would come my way and help lead me out of the darkness that surrounds me."

She laughs to herself quietly, "Remember that whole fate thing… I think it's been you I've been waiting for."

She turns slightly in my arms, finds my lips, and kisses me deeply.

"There's no doubt in my mind that fate brought us together," I say while gripping her waist tightly, staring into those beautiful blue eyes of hers.

"I think you're going to like what I have in store for you tonight," she purrs before kissing me softly.

The cocky smirk on my face says there's nothing I'm more sure of as Ashley takes my hand in hers, motioning for me to follow her.

We walk out onto the hotel balcony where an ice bucket and champagne are waiting next to a plush, tall back chair.

She motions for me to sit down as she drops to her knees in front of me.

Ashley undoes the button on my jeans when it hits me. She's recreating my Masqued fantasy! *Shit, if I didn't know it already, I certainly know it now. I love this girl with everything I have.*

I grab her chin while she frees my throbbing cock. "Ashley, you are so fucking perfect. You drive me crazy."

She looks up at me with a deviant smirk on her face. "Good thing because you do the same to me... Oh, and please call me Maggie."

The End

Sneak Peek

Read on for a Sneak Peek of Lottie and Greyson's book
Make You Love Me…

Make You Love Me

My Love,

Where do I begin?

I want you to know that you mean the absolute world to me. Filling even my saddest days with rays of sun. The way you hold me just right and know exactly what my body and mind need whenever you are near.

I can't believe it has been over 2 years and you still evoke butterflies every time I see you. I sometimes think I can feel your loving gaze even when you're not around.

Thank you for loving me even through my ups and downs and let's be real there have been more downs than ups lately. You have stayed by my side through the endless doctor appointments and treatments. Always smiling and making me feel beautiful and loved.

Even at my lowest, you empower me to be strong. You are my rock, which I am eternally thankful for.

But what about you and your life? I need to know that you will be okay even when I am no longer around. Living the life of a normal 18-year-old guy, with a future filled with endless possibilities.

Before you argue, I want you to know I have put some serious thought into this, and this is what I want for you.

I want you to be happy.

I want you to have a loving family filled with gorgeous, smiling children and the life you always dreamed about. Owning your own shop, designing, and seeing your sketches come to life.

I won't be able to give you those things, of that, I am sure. You deserve the world because that is what you gave me every day, selflessly.

You have touched my soul with your love, and for that, I will always be grateful. I don't think I would have made it through this past year without you.

This is probably the hardest thing I have ever had to do. To tell the man I love with all my heart and soul that this is the end...

I know this will come as a shock, but I'm leaving town. By the time you read this, I will already be gone. Don't come looking for me... it's better this way.

Just know I've gone to live out the rest of my time, however long that may be, with a heart filled with your love.

I want you to wake up every day and feel my love surround you, even if I am not there.

You will get past this and find a girl who will love you for the amazing man you are. Because you deserve that. You deserve everything. I'm just sorry it couldn't be with me.

I'm doing this because I love you and I hope you never forget that.

Love Always,

Your Everything 🖤

Afterword

Thank you so much for reading Make You Miss Me. It means the world to us to have your support.

Reviews are everything to us authors. So, if you enjoyed reading, please consider leaving a review!

We have so much in store for our readers…
Sign up for our Newsletter so you don't miss out on book news or new releases.

Acknowledgments

Thank you to my ride or die, LOML, my husband, for always supporting me and loving me through everything. Also, for the writing inspo :)

Shout out to my toddler for entertaining herself when I needed to fit in some writing and for inspiring me to be the best version of me.

Thank you to my book bestie now co-author for riding this wild roller coaster with me and being the other part of my brain. Let's make magic together, babe!

-A

I want to thank my husband for dealing with my many late nights filled with writing and unwatched shows. Thank you for believing in this crazy dream of mine.

Thank you to my children for understanding that "I need just a few more minutes" really means "until I get this scene finished." You two are the reason I'm shooting for the stars.

Eeep! My other half, thank you for doing this with me. We make one kick ass team and I'm so proud of what we've accomplished so far. This is only the beginning!

xox - L

Cindy, thank you for every encouraging word and piece of advice along the way... Your ability to decipher our crazy babble is top-notch. Thanks for being our O.G. ride or die! We love you!

Shannon, thank you for being as direct & honest as you are supportive & excited throughout this journey! Your proofreading and keen eye played a major part in our writing adventure. We appreciate you and all the encouragement.

To our Beta team, Trisha, Corinne, Tegan, Melissa, Tanya and Jennifer… Thank you for dedicating the time to read our novella and giving us feedback to make it the best debut we could!

Thank you to our ARC team. We appreciate each of you for taking your time to give us an honest review and promote our book. Reviews help authors more than people realize and we are so grateful.

TL Swan, not only would we not have met because of your readers' group, but we also wouldn't have been so encouraged to be authors. Thank you to Tee and the fellow cygnets for all the advice and constant motivation to go for it!!

We also want to thank Author Danda K for all her help and patience with us newbie authors!

Last but certainly not least, we want to give a shout out to our Book Obsessed Babes community...

Each of you inspired us throughout this amazing journey.

Thank you all for being a part of something that we cherish, we're truly thankful.

About the Author

A New Yorker and a Southern Belle.
Two Book Obsessed Babes that became lifelong best friends over their love for a good romance novel.

When they're not writing, they're devouring a good book or spending time with their family and friends.
Total opposites in some ways and exactly the same in others, making them a dynamic author duo.

Let's keep in touch...

Follow us on Instagram
www.instagram.com/lashaw.author
Join our Facebook Reader Group
www.facebook.com/groups/bookobsessedbabes/
TikTok
www.tiktok.com/@bookobsessedbabes

Also By

Make You Series

#0.5 Make You Miss Me (Trent & Ashley)

#1 Make You Love Me (Greyson & Lottie)

#2 M.Y.W.M (Emerson & Nox)- Pre Order

Reckless Hearts Series

#1 Reckless Abandon (Sloan & Wesley)

#2 Reckless Impulse (Eli & Quinn)- Pre-Order

Wild Blooms Series

Blossom & Bliss (Blossom & Dalton)

Made in United States
Troutdale, OR
12/28/2023